MURDER IN CHAMPAGNE SHORES

MURDER IN CHAMPAGNE SHORES

AMIE DENMAN

WORLDWIDE

TORONTO • NEW YORK • LONDON
AMSTERDAM • PARIS • SYDNEY • HAMBURG
STOCKHOLM • ATHENS • TOKYO • MILAN
MADRID • WARSAW • BUDAPEST • AUCKLAND

WORLDWIDE™

Recycling programs for this product may not exist in your area.

ISBN-13: 978-1-335-73630-7

Murder in Champagne Shores

First published in 2020 by Amie Denman.
This edition published in 2021.

Copyright © 2020 by Amie Denman

This edition published by arrangement with Harlequin Books S.A.

For questions and comments about the quality of this book, please contact us at CustomerService@Harlequin.com.

Harlequin Enterprises ULC
22 Adelaide St. West, 40th Floor
Toronto, Ontario M5H 4E3, Canada
www.ReaderService.com

Printed in U.S.A.

Dear Reader,

After writing three dozen romance novels, I've decided to murder people. Fictionally, of course! When I began my publication journey, my first few romances also included a mystery element. I grew up reading Agatha Christie's books and watching *Murder, She Wrote*, and I love the cozy mystery genre. So, I'm circling back to where I began.

Writing *Murder in Champagne Shores* was so much fun that I plan to write a series based on my sleuth, Millie Silver, and her friends in the Florida beach community of Champagne Shores. I hope you'll love this book and check back for more.

Happy reading,
Amie

ONE

MY LIFE IS like roller skating down a rainbow waving a paintbrush. I own the True Colors Paint Store in Champagne Shores, Florida, and everyone in my small town comes to me for advice when they want to repaint a bathroom, their porch, their mother-in-law suite, or even their doghouse. You can't take chances on choosing the right paint color.

My relationship with color started very young when I declared war on my aunt's living room. That room had beautiful windows, comfortable furniture, and an atmosphere of love, but it did not want to be green. I told her the room had reached out to me for help, and she patiently drove me to the big home improvement store in Jacksonville so I could save her living room from being trapped in its lettuce green cage. That trip changed my life. Standing before the wall of paint sample cards, all of them for the taking, I had found my religion.

"It's here," my sister Tiffany said, bursting through the front door of my paint store. "The new summer display!"

My yellow Labrador Sunshine hopped up and greeted Tiffany with a swipe of her tongue across Tiffany's knee. I ran an elbow across my sales counter, shoving papers and clutter into an empty box at the end. Tiffany unrolled a long poster and we both held down an end.

"Beautiful," I breathed. "Look at the gradient from hot to cool."

Like me, Tiffany loves color and painting. She just works in a different medium. At her salon next door to my paint shop, she helps customers choose hair and nail colors to make them look more beautiful but not as if they're trying too hard. Our Aunt Minerva is her biggest cheerleader and spokesperson with the prettiest set of highlights in Champagne Shores.

"I love summer," my sister said.

"It's March," our brother Darwin commented from the paint mixing counter in the back of the store. "Tomorrow is the spring equinox which is the first day of spring." At twenty-one, Darwin was the youngest of the three of us and always the most literal. Whereas Tiffany and I saw the world in colorful detail, Darwin was a black and white kind of guy.

"Retail," Tiffany said, rolling her eyes. "We plan ahead."

"You don't have to plan for summer," he said. "It starts at the summer equinox whether you put up a fingernail paint chart or not." He tilted his head and frowned. "Is there some reason why nail polish colors change with the seasons?"

Tiffany and I exchanged a smile. "No," I said, "people just like change."

He nodded as if he was processing that thought. "Okay."

Tiffany and I went back to examining her poster which I knew from experience she would hang right where her customers would have to stare at it as they waited for their hair color to take hold. They wouldn't be able to resist getting their nails done, too.

Champagne Shores could best be described as an Old Florida town along the Atlantic Coast. It was the kind of town where tourists could expect to buy big bags of oranges at a roadside market along with kitschy souvenirs to take home to the grandkids. Atlantic Avenue stretched along the coastline and was home to shops like my paint store and my sister's beauty parlor. There was also a cozy brewpub, a family restaurant, a locally owned grocery store, a coffee shop and bakery, an antiques store, a post office and a seasonal fruit vendor in a rustic but pretty fruit stand.

The side streets of Champagne Shores were home to the police and fire stations, a few value-priced motels, a drugstore, gas station and convenience store, and aging but decently maintained homes. There were a few grand old homes from an era of enthusiastic development sparked by the railroad, and most of those had been lucky enough to escape being divided up into apartments.

The entire town seemed balanced on the brink of Old Florida with its sleepy beach town vibe and Modern Florida with its lust for catering to tourists. The two massive hotels on the beach owned by corporations were evidence that the town was going to have to embrace the idea of getting with the tourist program. When a national chain had put up the SunBeam and SunStar Resorts, blocking the view of the ocean from some of the older businesses and homes, there had been an uproar. The noise subsided when those resorts also brought good jobs to town so local residents didn't have to make the twenty-five-minute drive to Jacksonville to make minimum wage.

"The names of these nail colors are wonderful," I

said, putting my finger on the poster. "Beach baby is a perfect name for this peachy pink, and I love Former Wallflower Red. The name says a lot."

Tiffany looked at my nails. "Chipped," she said. "And you've been picking."

"I'm nervous," I admitted. "I'm meeting Ransom Heyward tomorrow morning to go over paint colors for his new development. If he likes my choices, I may get the contract to supply all the paint, interior and exterior. He has fifty vacation villas planned in the first wave of construction and potentially another fifty after that. Do you know how many gallons of paint that is?"

I saw Darwin's head come up and he stopped his paint shaker. "What is the square footage of each home?" he asked.

I knew from experience he had a calculator in his brain that would produce the exact number of gallons if he fed it enough information.

"I don't know," I said. "That's one of the many things I need to find out. But I do know it's a whole lot of paint and the revenue from it would be enough to renovate our apartments upstairs."

"You shouldn't be nervous about your meeting with Ransom," Tiffany said. "If he's asking you, he must have heard about your reputation. He hasn't worked with any other local businesses, so it's quite an honor."

I laughed. "I don't think honor is the word they'll use at the coffee shop or brewpub. Ransom Heyward is the least popular man in town."

"I just wish he had a wife or a girlfriend. I could use someone new to work on," Tiffany said. "And she would probably want the works."

"Tourists," I said. "If his vacation rentals go as

planned, there'll be hundreds of new people coming to town starting next spring. Maybe they'll need a new look while they're on vacation."

"Unless he puts in his own beauty shop, the jerk," she grumbled.

People in town were irritated with Ransom Heyward because, despite the millions he was pouring into an oceanfront development, residents of Champagne Shores felt they were being robbed. Ransom was using contractors from out of state to build the dozens of vacation villas, dig the central pond and fountain, and create his own small commercial village. The village part really burned the biscuits of local business owners. His development would have its own coffee shop, souvenir shop, beach rental, restaurant, bar, and even bookstore.

Luckily for me, tourists don't buy paint on vacation anyway. And, luckily for me, mine was the only business in town he was considering using. I couldn't put a finger on exactly why except that the mayor's wife may have recommended my instincts for color and, perhaps, the fact that I had chosen to be nice to the guy.

He wasn't a total ogre, despite what people in town thought. He hadn't been completely demanding and stubborn.

"I'm meeting him Monday morning," I said. "At his office on location in the model house. It's all done except for the carpet, paint, and furniture, so now it's the fun part."

As if on cue, Ransom Heyward walked past my shop on the sunny Saturday morning.

"Sheesh," Tiffany said. "He needs layers. It looks like someone used safety scissors to cut his hair."

Ransom had passed by, but we watched him backtrack and lean into the front window, peering inside. He was tall and dark haired, probably somewhere in his mid-fifties, and a bachelor according to local gossip. I waved and he took it as an invitation. He began talking as soon as he walked through my front door, not pausing to determine if he might be interrupting me or someone else. Sunshine greeted him at the door, but she didn't give him a friendly lick. Instead, she stood at attention, head cocked.

"A reporter from the Jacksonville paper will be there on Monday morning to take pictures of you helping me."

He was a man without preamble. I'd noticed it before. He began trains of thought right in the middle of the train as if whoever he was talking to already knew about the engine and the first three cars.

"Why?" I asked.

"Good for my reputation," he said, not bothering to hide a smirk. "Apparently, I've been criticized in the local watering holes for not working with any locals, so this will be my proof I'm not the villain people seem to think I am."

"Maybe this will be bad for my reputation," I joked. "Meeting with you and having witnesses."

"But good for your bank account," he said. "I've discovered that when people are forced to choose between the two, money always wins. See you at eight on Monday."

After dropping that little insult to my character, he left without another word.

"He's probably not wrong," Darwin commented.

I crossed my arms and glared at my brother. "How would you like to go along and make nice with the reporter? Maybe you could pose for some pictures and give lots of effusive quotes for the newspaper article."

I knew I'd landed a hit to his entire central nervous system when he visibly flinched. Darwin, despite his level of genius, did not engage in unnecessary conversation, did not like to be hugged or touched or even ride in small cars with other humans. I often wondered what was happening in his brain, but I was left to assume it was some kind of nuclear calculus I couldn't even find a color for.

"I can't," he said. "I'm upgrading our operating system Sunday night. It could take hours and you never know if you'll hit on a stable channel of the newest software. There could be bugs. Patches. Security updates. Can't take chances with our life's blood computer system."

Calling our computer system our life's blood was the closest Darwin ever came to hyperbole.

"If the reporter is attractive, text me and I'll bring you the samples you forgot," Tiffany said.

I laughed. "You know in advance that I'll forget some?"

"Imagination is my life's blood," she said, grinning at Darwin. "I'm going to go next door and tape this up without even measuring, just going to eyeball it."

Another quiver from Darwin. "I'll be right there," he said.

Sunshine and I followed them outside so I could watch the show through Tiffany's glass windows. I knew from experience that my brother would measure down from the ceiling, across from intersecting walls, and up from the floor just to make sure that poster of nail colors was perfectly level and square.

"And you should wear something nice," Ransom Heyward said, appearing out of nowhere as I was busy snooping in the beauty shop's front windows. He made me jump and I put a hand over my heart. "That apron doesn't do a thing for you."

He pointed to my painter's apron with the name of my shop on the front. My name, Millie Silver, had been lovingly embroidered by my Aunt Minerva. Even though I frequently washed it, the once-white apron was now a museum exhibit of the colors I'd helped people choose and paint over the past three years of owning my store. At twenty-five, I was proud of my success, and I didn't give a paint stirring stick what Ransom thought of my appearance.

I raised an eyebrow at him and he took a step backward. "The interior designer I've worked with on other projects thinks it's a mistake to go with a local. He says you're too close to the project, and what we need to sell in vacation rentals is the fantasy. People want to feel at home without feeling like they're at home."

The man truly was irritating. I put my hands on my hips. "I think I'm smart enough to know that," I said. I bit my tongue before I continued my tirade, and we faced off in a moment of silence before Ransom turned on his heel and walked away without a word.

Hazel Hayes from the bakery across the street leaned out her front door. "Is he gone?" she stage-whispered.

I shrugged. It wasn't my job to keep track of the guy. Hazel looked both ways and hurried across the street on her short legs. She always reminded me of an adorable puppy that wanted to be loved by everyone. She was a few years older than I was and had taken over the bakery and coffee shop from a former owner who fell in love with a sailor and took off to live on a boat and travel the world.

Given Hazel's luck with men, I doubted she would be taking off anytime soon, even though she commanded an excellent view of Atlantic Drive when she stood on a box behind her bakery counter.

"You two had quite an argument," she said, leaning down and slipping a treat to Sunshine. "I saw the whole thing. I'll bet you really told him off."

"What?" I said. I'd said one sentence, although I couldn't claim it was exactly an audition for a Miss Florida Congeniality run.

"We all hate him," she hissed.

"I don't hate him," I said. "He's just used to getting what he wants."

She cocked her head. "He could be a whole lot nicer about it. And it wouldn't kill him to buy a dozen cupcakes for his construction crew every now and then."

She scurried back across the street and dashed into her bakery where I knew she would return to being sweetness and light. Maybe other people in town were capable of holding onto a grudge, but Hazel let things blow away like powdered sugar. The local motel owners were another story, and so was the homeowner's association. Even the local library had put up a carefully worded fight on behalf of the historical society housed in its basement when Ransom had torn down an entire street of homes that some people considered historic despite their outdated siding and sorrowful shrubbery.

Ransom Heyward brought out the villain in even the nicest people. He didn't usually get under my skin much because I tended to be more…ahem…direct than sweet Hazel, my slightly eccentric aunt, and my sunshiny sister. Maybe that was why Darwin was comfortable working for me. Reading between the lines wasn't his personal strength.

My Aunt Minerva stopped by the paint store late on Saturday afternoon. She had a big shopping bag with her, and I guessed the contents even before she opened it behind the counter and invited me to peek in.

"I need your help with color," she said.

This was a surprise. Whereas I had the color magic with paint, and my sister had it with nails and hair, Aunt Minerva had color juju when it came to yarn. She could choose a yarn color with the same kind of intuition I used to determine whether a laundry room could be mint green without feeling like a toothpaste accident.

I looked in the bag which was, predictably, filled with skeins of yarn.

"I don't know who will win it," she said. Despite her perfectly colored hair, my aunt's wrinkles revealed her age and time spent in the Florida sun. The line between her eyebrows deepened and she looked devastated by her inability to choose.

"What are you making?"

"A beach bag. I'm donating it to the gift basket the tourist board is putting together for the annual festival next week."

Calling the festival annual was a stretch. This would only be the second year for the glorified street fair the town council thought would put Champagne Shores on the spring break tourist radar. There would be food trucks and even a few carnival rides set up in the city parking lot by the beach, and photos from last year's first attempt were on the city's website and brochures. I'd seen the pictures, and it was clear to me they were improved upon by modern technology, but I couldn't argue with the need to bring in revenue. The town's leadership was floating plans for a pier stretching into the Atlantic with bars and restaurants just like some other towns along the coast.

"It will be a nice donation to the cause," I said, reaching into the bag and pulling out an especially pretty shade of ocean blue.

"But I don't know who will win it," my aunt said, her voice filled with distress. "You know I choose colors based on the person. I've never made an anonymous project before. What if a hothead or a plain jane or a widow or a horse trader wins it? The color could be all wrong, a disaster."

"You could go with neutral," I said.

"You and I both know there's no such thing," she said, scandal in her tone.

This was true, despite what the magazines and paint charts said, I refused to believe there was a color that didn't deserve to be called a color.

"Stripes," I declared. "It's cheating, but it solves your problem."

"How—"

"Four colors. Red, white, blue, yellow. One for every personality type and also very cheerful and beachy."

Aunt Minerva smiled. "You've put my mind at rest. Now don't be too nice to that nasty developer when you see him on Monday."

"How did you know about that?"

"Everyone knows. This is Champagne Shores."

EVEN THOUGH I usually take Sundays off and enjoy the beach or bicycling around town, I worked in my paint store unboxing and organizing inventory. There were plenty of cans of white flat, satin, semi-gloss and gloss on hand, and all those cans were just waiting to become one of the thousands of colors my customers could choose from. Within reason, of course, and with good advice. There were some colors that were never meant to be on walls—a fact I hadn't always been successful convincing people to believe.

After a long day of restocking brushes, drop cloths, rollers, tape, and other painting supplies, I took a bike ride down the strip of stores and restaurants that made up my hometown. I used to dread seeing the cross street I had named *the street of sad homes* when I was a kid. Ransom Heyward had removed all the homes on that street and there was now construction fencing around a sizable piece of real estate on the southern edge of Champagne Shores.

For dinner, I microwaved leftovers in my apartment above the paint store, enjoying the solitude. Darwin and Tiffany also lived above the building that houses my paint store and Tiffany's beauty shop, but the area was divided so we each had our own space. Our apartments were outdated, but the clever application of paint colors made them homey and nice. My Aunt Minerva and Uncle Foster had lovingly conserved the life insurance money our parents left us, and Tiffany and I had used our share to buy the building three years ago.

On Monday morning, I was up early. Sunshine trotted alongside my bike, looking excited about having an outing on a weekday. She didn't need a leash, and everyone in town knew my three-year-old dog whose name matched her color. A red compact car passed me on the quiet early-morning street and pulled in the entrance to the King's Ransom Vacation Development just ahead of me.

The reporter. As I'd lain in bed the night before, I'd thought about how to handle being someone else's PR stunt. It seemed to me that my best bet was to be my own PR machine and promote the True Colors Paint Store. The red car parked in front of the model home where there was already a black Mercedes that everyone in town would recognize. It had Florida license plates, but Ransom never seemed like a Florida native to anyone in Champagne Shores.

He was too busy remaking Florida into the image he thought tourists wanted to see, and they all knew he'd move on to the next Florida town with land for sale as soon as this project was over.

"Good morning," the reporter said as he approached, a camera in one hand and his other extended in a friendly greeting.

I got off my bike and put down the kickstand. Sunshine made the first overture and sniffed the reporter's knees.

"Millie Silver," I said, shaking hands. "I own the True Colors Paint Store in Champagne Shores, and my specialty is helping people find just the right color for everything."

"Matt Riley," he said. He was taller than I was and had sandy brown hair and blue eyes. He also had a nice smile. "Maybe you should help me with the house I just bought. The former owners painted every room the same color."

"On-sale painters," I said, nodding. "I know the type."

He gave me a curious look.

"You know, the paint color must have been on sale, so they bought it all. Maybe someone special ordered it and never picked it up, or there was a mistake at the factory, or just a glut in the market for…"

"Peach," he said. "The whole house looks like a frozen drink on a cruise ship."

"I can help you," I said.

I'd run into on-sale painters before and, over the years, I'd developed a theory about almost any painter you could name. Revenge painters who chose exterior colors to irritate their neighbors, magazine spreaders who wanted to imitate what they saw on the glossy pages, timid painters afraid of color, and their total opposites who were blatantly irresponsible with hues.

"So where's our host?" he asked.

"Inside?"

We walked up the front sidewalk of the model home with Sunshine at our heels. I hadn't been consulted about the siding color of the model vacation home, but I couldn't argue with the soft buttery yellow and white trim. It was a classic, certain not to clash with other homes or landscaping.

Matt knocked, and we waited. Sunshine investigated the porch and then wandered down into the front yard which was mostly still mud in the construction zone. I rang the doorbell and then turned so I could keep an eye on my dog. Sunshine was ears up, tail up, staring at the gracefully curving pond that was planned as a central water feature for the vacation development. The plans called for a fountain, swim float and paddle boards, but there was something already floating in the pond that looked out of place.

"What's that?" I asked, pointing at the object in the middle of the pond. It looked…odd.

Sunshine began barking and running toward the water. Being a Labrador Retriever, she loved getting her feet and every other part of her wet.

"Wait," I yelled. "Sunshine!"

Too late. She was already in the water, swimming madly toward the floating object in the middle, her yellow coat contrasting with the dark water.

Matt raised his camera and zoomed in. He gasped and dropped the camera. His face turned four shades of white I could have named if I'd taken the time, and then I realized what I was looking at.

"Is it…a body?"

Sunshine had nearly reached the floating object, and Matt picked up his camera from the ground. I assumed he hit record mode because I didn't hear any clicking and he didn't move. My dog took the body's arm in her mouth and began swimming back to shore with her treasure.

Despite my horror, I regretted that I didn't have a treat with me. Surely a dog who hauls in a human body deserves one? I didn't want her to become cynical.

"This is unbelievable," Matt whispered. "I'm recording it all. Your dog is swimming in with what looks like a body." *I wondered what on earth else he thought he could be.* We walked toward the water's edge, Matt still recording as he moved slowly and steadily.

Sunshine backed onto the shore, dragging what she had retrieved. Matt and I stared at the body of Ransom Heyward, floating faceup and obviously dead.

TWO

I CALLED THE police and held onto Sunshine's collar while Matt examined the body. He held his camera out in one hand and gently poked at Ransom with the other. I wanted to ask him what he planned to do with the recording because it would clearly make the world's worst social media post.

"Dead," he said. "Very."

"Don't touch him," I said. "I mean, not any more."

"Touch who?" the dispatcher asked as she came on the line.

"The body," I explained. I recognized the voice of Gladys who had worked at the police station my entire life, and I told her I was at King's Ransom with a dead body. She gasped and said she'd send someone right away.

"Do you think it was an accident?" Matt asked when I'd slid my phone back in my pocket. "Maybe he fell in and drowned?"

I shrugged, unwilling to tell a reporter about the dozens of people who would not be disappointed to hear of Ransom's untimely demise. Immediately, I pictured the good people of Champagne Shores raising a glass at Cecil's Brewpub or indulging in extra icing on their cinnamon rolls at the bakery when they heard the news.

"He could have had a heart attack," Matt said.

I admired the guy for his determination not to think

ill of his fellow man. I guessed he didn't know that much about the deceased's relationships with others.

"It's a big pond, though," Matt continued, shading his eyes and scanning the shore at the other end. "Maybe there's a killer down there hiding a murder weapon and laughing gleefully."

So much for his faith in humanity. Even a seemingly nice guy like Matt could get his feathers ruffled by finding a corpse out on an assignment. It wasn't my cup of tea, either.

Chief Parker was the first to arrive. He used the flashing lights and the siren, basically a signal to the entire town that something was going down. The last time Carl Parker had gone emergency with his police car was a false alarm the time Poppy Russell saw the space shuttle take off from down the coast and thought the Russians were invading. She had all her cats in a bomb shelter when the Chief arrived and had to talk her out of her cellar.

Given the calamity of the situation, I wasn't surprised to see the mayor's street-legal golf cart roll in just behind the Chief. Mayor Maurice Bell's custom royal blue metallic golf cart with beach tires was a common sight in Champagne Shores. I'd suggested the color. Flashy, but still masculine. The shiny aluminum wheels were his choice after our consultation, but I couldn't blame a guy for trying to relive his youth. His wife Irene kept her youth alive with regular trips to my sister's salon.

The Chief barreled out of his patrol car and stared at the body lying on the muddy shore of the pond. Ransom's expensive leather shoes were in the water, but the rest of him was drying out in the early morning Florida sun. Chief Parker looked stoic but puzzled. When the mayor got out of his golf cart and laid eyes on the body, he looked as if he was going to lose his breakfast. The rest of the police department, both of them, arrived moments later in the town's other police car. After a quick look at the scene, one of them ran back to the car and returned with a roll of yellow caution tape.

"Just what do you think you're going to do with that?" Chief Parker said.

"Standard procedure."

The chief raised his eyes to the sky. "Maybe we'll ask a few questions and begin an investigation before we tangle ourselves up in tape."

"Sorry," the younger officer said. "It's my first murder."

"No one's said anything about a murder," Mayor Bell said. "Not in scenic tourist-friendly Champagne Shores."

Chief Parker knelt and took a closer look at Ransom's head. "It'll be up to a medical examiner to determine, but I think it's safe to say he had some help getting into this pond. Maybe a club or a big stick."

We all stared at each other, the ugly realization that we were in the presence of ice-cold murder freezing us into an odd tableau of people.

"My dog already defiled the scene," I said. "Sunshine can't fight her retriever instincts, and she's a great swimmer. She towed...uh... Ransom in." I wasn't sure what to call a dead body, even though I knew him and had just talked to him yesterday. "In case the medical examiner finds teeth marks on the body," I finished, risking babbling and somehow incriminating myself or my dog for murder. Sunshine wasn't interested in the investigation. She had shaken off all the pond water and was lying in the grass drying out.

Chief Parker chewed the inside of his lip and ran a hand over his bald head. "I retired from Tallahassee to get away from crap like this." He turned to me. "You should go, and I'll be by your store later to take your statement."

"Do you think he was really murdered?" I whispered as the chief walked me over to my bicycle, not wanting to air any more Champagne Shores dirty laundry in front of the Jacksonville reporter than was necessary. He'd seen plenty already, and I could only imagine how this article was going to play on the front page of the paper.

Chief Parker leaned closer. "I don't think he crushed the back of his own skull. I only saw the edge of the wound, but it wasn't pretty."

I felt a little sick imagining what the back of Ransom's head might look like, so I took the chief's advice and gripped my bicycle handlebars, ready to escape. I glanced back at the ugly scene with a sick feeling of distaste, and the chief caught me. Maybe my color was more in the putrid green area of the paint palette than the blush pink.

"Mayor," the chief said, "think you could give Millie a ride to her shop in your golf cart? She looks a little on the queasy side."

The mayor looked even unhappier than everyone else at the scene, and I remembered the nice things he'd said about Ransom Heyward as he'd tried to plead the new development's case. Aside from me, the mayor was probably the only person who didn't hate the murder victim and may even have liked him a little bit.

"Sure," Maurice Bell said, looking ashen. "Come on, Millie."

I put my bicycle on the back, and Sunshine and I climbed in the golf cart. Neither of us spoke as we drove out of the unfinished development. The only completed house was the model one, and I wondered what would happen to the entire project now that Ransom was suddenly and inexplicably dead. He was a bachelor without any family that I knew of. Would his project be completed, sold, or become an eyesore and terrible reminder of what had happened?

I looked at the floor of the mayor's prized golf cart and immediately felt compunction. The shiny black floor was a mess of mud, already dried in the Florida heat.

"Sorry," I said. "Sunshine got your cart all muddy."

He looked down and his expression hardened for a moment. He grunted something that sounded like "that's okay," and he didn't say anything for the next two minutes until he dropped me off in front of my paint store.

"You're done already?" Darwin asked when I came through the door. "You said you'd be gone all morning. It's," he consulted his smart watch, "eight forty-two."

"Change of plans. Ransom wasn't able to review my paint swatches."

"Too busy?"

"Too dead," I said. "When the reporter and I got there, we found him floating in his pond."

My brother Darwin had never been accused of being overly emotional in his life. He regarded the world scientifically and believed that the only mysteries of the universe were the ones science hadn't got around to explaining. Yet.

"Two things," he said. "Your dog is wet, and no one dies from floating."

"Sunshine retrieved the body, and Chief Parker said it appeared a blow to the back of the head killed Ransom, not a morning swim."

"That makes sense," Darwin said. "I'm going to calibrate the paint shaker because I think its timer is off. It may need a firmware update."

Tiffany flung open my front door and it slammed into a life-sized cardboard cutout of a woman smiling and holding a paint can. The paper woman landed face down on the floor and we all stared at it.

"I think it needs a counterbalance," Darwin said. "To prevent that sort of thing."

Tiffany opened her mouth in outrage. "This sort of thing only happens when I hear a rumor that my sister was at a murder scene. Is it really true?"

"How do you already know about that? Ransom Heyward has been dead for thirty minutes."

"You don't know that," my brother said. "You found him forty-four minutes ago, assuming you were on time for your meeting, but he could have been dead for hours, even days."

I sucked in my lips and breathed through my hose. "We just saw him Saturday morning."

"That was two—" Darwin began.

"Enough," I yelled. "The man is dead, I don't know for how long, but I do know somebody killed him."

Tiffany took my hand and we both sat on the stools by the counter where giant books of decorating ideas and hundreds of pages of paint samples laid open for customers to peruse.

"I heard about it from Poppy who called the police station when the chief went blaring past. She was afraid it was the Russians again, but Gladys the dispatcher tried talking her down and somehow revealed the whole story instead."

"She came to your shop?"

"No, she went straight to the bakery, but she obviously left home in a hurry because she only had one cat in her purse. She's still over there talking to Hazel and feeding her cat pieces of apple turnover."

"I can't believe Ransom is dead," I said.

"Somebody must have wished on a big set of birthday candles," Tiffany said.

"That would make it easy to solve," Darwin commented. "The police should simply review birth records and determine who had a birthday between Saturday morning and this morning."

My sister and I rolled our eyes at Darwin.

"It's just a figure of speech," I said.

He looked as if he didn't believe me and went back to placing tiny weights on the paint shaker and observing it. Tiffany and I sat silently for a few minutes, and I soothed my frayed nerves by flipping through charts of beautiful colors and imagining walls and furniture wearing a coat of paint that suited them.

"Who do you think did it?" Tiffany asked.

I shrugged. The question had been on my mind since the moment I realized his death was not an accident. "Someone who wanted him dead."

"Which is everyone," my sister said.

"It's not everyone," I said. "Did you want him dead?"

The door to my shop opened slowly and Chief Parker stood in it, filling the doorframe with his round figure.

"I, UH, WANTED TO ASK you a few questions," the police chief said. If he overheard me asking Tiffany if she wanted the victim dead, he apparently wasn't going to mention it. To her credit, Tiffany doesn't seem like a murderer, and the worst thing she'd said about the deceased was a critique of his haircut when he passed by on Saturday morning.

Plenty of people in Champagne Shores had said far worse things, and I imagined the news of Ransom Heyward's death was spreading like a hurricane wind over town and causing quite a few people to do a mental rewind of all the rotten things they'd said and thought.

"Go ahead," I said. "It's okay to interrogate me in front of Darwin and Tiffany. I'll tell them everything anyway."

"It's not an interrogation, and you're not a suspect," he said. "Unless you're planning to hand me an easy win late in my career and confess to the crime."

I shook my head and pointed to a seat. Some police officers might be intimidating, but I'd been inside Chief Parker's home and knew him through his color choices. Two years earlier, I'd chosen paint colors for every room in the house he and his wife bought when they moved to Champagne Shores. Although he looked like a classic cop with his buzz cut and deep wrinkles around his eyes suggesting he'd seen it all, I'd discovered he had a penchant for bright colors. The Parker residence would have looked like a lollipop factory if I hadn't suggested subtle ways of toning it down. It turned out to be cheerful and inviting without going full carnival.

Chief Parker sat on the third stool so he was on my right and my sister on my left. Darwin hummed the theme from a science fiction movie and appeared to be tuning us all out. "What time did you arrive on the murder scene this morning?"

"A few minutes before eight, maybe five 'til," I said, taking a glance at Darwin whose slight twitch showed me he was recalculating what he'd said earlier.

"And was the reporter from the Jacksonville paper already there?"

"Yes, but I saw him pull in. He passed me on the street in his car and parked just as I was putting the kickstand down on my bike. So he couldn't have done it."

The chief raised an eyebrow. "That doesn't mean he couldn't have done it."

"Okay," I said. I had no experience with murder, investigations, or questions from cops who'd clearly rather be writing tickets for jaywalking from the beach parking lot to the surfboard rental shack. Matt Riley seemed like a nice guy, and I would bet my paint chart he was just as shocked as I was when we discovered the body, but I couldn't blame the chief for keeping his suspect list open.

"And then what happened?"

"We—I—knocked on the door, no one answered, so we—he—rang the bell and then Sunshine went off sniffing and we heard her barking at the pond." I was proud of myself for reporting the events in great detail. My dog sat next to me and raised her head when she heard her name. I kissed her nose and told her she wasn't in trouble.

"Did you see the body at that point?" the chief asked.

"I saw something in the pond, but I didn't know if it was a dead body or a flock of ducks."

The chief paused with his pen over his notepad. "Those two things wouldn't look anything alike, even from a distance."

"It's a figure of speech," Darwin said.

My genius brother had either developed a sense of humor at the least appropriate time or he felt the police chief had even less social awareness than he did and Darwin wanted to help the poor sucker out.

I was just disappointed that my detailed reporting had broken down like a trampled sand sculpture.

Patiently, the chief continued asking questions and making notes. *Was I his first interview or had he already asked the reporter all these questions?* We went over the part where my dog swam out and latched onto the body and then the brief interval between my phone call to the police and their arrival. I hoped my story matched Matt's, or we'd both end up looking either irresponsible or suspicious.

"What did you find after I left with the mayor?" I asked. Even though I was glad to get a ride back to my store and get away from the ugly scene, I was curious about what I'd missed. Being the one to find the murder victim's body made me feel a hint of responsibility for him. How long would he have floated there before someone else came along and found him? Surely the construction crews would have shown up eventually.

"A smoking gun would have been nice," the chief said, "but we didn't find a murder weapon, at least not yet. Of course, with those two young clowns I've got working for me, I'm usually just glad when they find their way back to the police station." He sighed. "Lucky me, I'd end up with the only murder ever recorded in this town, and I've got a crew of two guys who've probably never broken the speed limit or had a cavity."

"Maybe they'll surprise you?" I suggested. I felt bad for Chief Parker. When he and his wife had moved to town, we'd all heard the story of his gout and how his stressful job had tempted him to eat rich foods that inflamed his bad toe and thickened his waistline. His wife was hoping the pleasant pace of Champagne Shores would add years to his life and subtract inches from his gun belt. She had fit in and taken a job at the antique store two blocks down. Half antiques and half a yarn store, my Aunt Minerva visited almost every day to finger the yarns and chat with the owner, April May, and her only employee Sheila Parker.

"The murder weapon's out there somewhere," the chief said.

"Do you have any evidence?" Tiffany asked. My sister had remained silent as the chief and I reviewed the events of the morning, and she finally jumped in with a spot-on question. As a cosmetologist, she was experienced in the fine art of keeping her ears open and nodding encouragement as her customers told her details they wouldn't tell their gynecologists. She'd often shared with me the gossip she heard while Darwin shook his head, disapproving of either her methods or the effusive personal details.

The chief sighed. "Muddy footprints on the shore on the far side. Looks like a tussle of some kind happened down there, and it's probably where the fatal blow was struck. The victim's socks were filthy and his shoes probably were, too, before the pond water washed off the leather. Whoever fought with Ransom Heyward and ultimately killed him might be in the market for a new pair of shoes."

"Can you make a concrete form of the prints left in the mud and find a matching sole mate somewhere?" Tiffany asked.

Darwin raised his head and caught my eye, and I knew he was wondering if sole mate was a figure of speech. I shook my head slightly, and he went back to his computer.

"That works on crime shows on television, but it's just a crap show out there, skid marks in the mud. We took pictures, but I think we're going to have to catch the murderer the old-fashioned way."

"Which is?"

"Wait for someone to open his big fat mouth," Chief Parker said. "In a town like this, it's a cop's best friend."

He hoisted himself off his stool. "If you happen to see a bloody crowbar anywhere or overhear a confession, give me a call. Darwin, any chance you could come by the station and take a look at our computer? It's saying something about an anti-virus update and asking me to click a box. I'm never sure if I should do it, or if it's some kind of a trap."

Darwin nodded and promised to come over later, and Chief Parker tucked his notepad in his shirt pocket. On his way out the door, he picked up my cardboard lady and set her back on her feet so she could continue smiling and advertising paint.

THREE

"He has a nephew," my Aunt Minerva said.

"Who has a nephew?" I asked.

"Had, I should say."

"Ransom Heyward?"

Aunt Minerva nodded. "He had a nephew, and that nephew is the heir to his entire estate," she said, her eyes round with excitement. "That's what I heard at the yarn store. Sheila Parker was working, and she said that's what her husband told her."

A day had gone by, and I was certain everyone in Champagne Shores had decided to freshen up the paint in their bathroom, mudroom, playroom, or pantry. Each person who popped in for samples had questions about a lot more than paint, and I was already tired of hearing the story of my discovery of the body. Like other travel-worn stories, mine was starting to sound more and more like fiction every time I heard it repeated back to me. Darwin pointed out that sales were up thirty-two percent over the previous day, so I did take comfort in that fact.

"And the nephew is coming to town. Maybe as soon as today," Aunt Minerva said.

"Oh, wow," I said, uncertain what I should say about that slice of information and how it would impact the investigation that seemed to be going everywhere at once. Each paint shopper who visited my store had a different theory, and there were as many suspects as there were seagulls defiling the light posts by the beach.

"I wonder what he'll have to say," Minerva said.

"I'm sure he'll be devastated about his uncle's death."

I hadn't heard of any relatives and the only personal information anyone seemed to know was that Ransom was a bachelor. He hadn't befriended anyone in town, and there were no family photos in his office in the model home the one time I had been in there. Unrepentant snoop that I am, I had cased his office for pictures when he'd stepped outside to talk to his construction foreman. No wife, no grandkids, no classic college graduation picture with caps and gowns and happy parents, and definitely no nephew. Not even a cat or dog picture. He was one lonely guy, and I could only hope his bank account kept him company.

"Huh," Minerva said. "Hard to imagine anyone being devastated unless he was a whole lot nicer in his personal life than he was in his business one. I heard the contractors were close to walking off the job after Ransom's demands at the end of last week. He wanted them to hurry the project along but didn't offer to pay them any extra. Maybe that's why you didn't see any around on Monday morning when you were there. He was lucky his greed didn't leave him to float in that pond forever."

I rubbed my forehead and then realized I probably had buttercream-colored paint on my hand from a sample card I was making. My aunt's comment made me realize what had been bothering me about the silent Monday morning construction scene. There were no contractors or other workers around. I wished there had been, because construction workers usually begin very early, especially with Florida heat, and they would certainly have been the ones to discover the body.

It would have saved me the icky memory of seeing my beloved dog towing in a corpse, and it would have also removed me from the center of the widespread curiosity storm hanging over Champagne Shores.

"Maybe they were on another job," I said.

"Maybe they supplied the murder weapon and left," Aunt Minerva said as she picked up a paper towel and rubbed the paint off my forehead. "I heard it was a blunt object and it hasn't been found. There are plenty of blunt objects on construction trucks."

I swished my lips to the side and stared down my aunt. "The police will figure it out."

She laughed. "Maybe Chief Parker, but those other two are better suited for being crossing guards in the school zone."

"I feel bad for Chief Parker. He came to this town for a quiet retirement job, and now he's investigating the murder of a wealthy and unpopular guy with very little help."

"Sheila is worried about him. You should help him," Aunt Minerva said. "You're very curious, you were there when the body was discovered, and you know everyone in town."

"I'm not a detective," I protested, "and I don't want to go anywhere near this case. It's messy, and it will probably destroy my faith in the good people of Champagne Shores."

"How would that happen?"

I laughed. "Already, I've heard fifteen theories. Worse yet, the gossips are more than happy to throw everyone else under the prison bus. Even if no one in town ends up being convicted, I swear they're out there convicting each other as if there's a prize to be first. No way," I concluded. "I'm staying out of it."

"I thought you liked him," my aunt sniffed.

"Chief Parker?"

"Well, yes, but also Ransom Heyward."

"I liked the potential of doing business with him and pouring that cash into my time-capsule of the nineteen-eighties living space." I pointed upstairs for emphasis even though my aunt knew where I lived. She'd been over for dinner at least once a week for several years, ever since I finished a two-year art degree and moved in upstairs. Tiffany and Darwin followed, and my aunt's house emptied out too fast to suit her. The weekly casserole shared at my kitchen table was her way of letting us know she loved us and making sure we ate vegetables. My Uncle Foster bowled once a week, so he missed out on casserole night, but he kept in close contact with all of us anyway.

"If I were murdered, I would expect you and your siblings to help the police night and day until you found my killer," my aunt said.

I smiled and looped an arm around my aunt's shoulders. "I can't imagine Ransom's nephew loved him as much as we love you, so you can't make a comparison like that, and you certainly can't want me to waste my time and energy snooping around Champagne Shores."

Aunt Minerva sat on a stool and flipped through my big book of room ideas with paint color suggestions. I knew she'd seen that book a dozen times, but it appeared she was going to park herself in my store and have another look.

"Thinking of redecorating?" I asked.

She turned a page. "Inspiration," she said.

Darwin came in through the back door and went straight to mission control where he mixed and tested paint colors. He had a rack of different kinds of lights ranging from LED to fluorescent, and his lectures on lumens could last an hour. Darwin's inability to read social cues often caused him to over-explain to customers foolish enough to ask if a paint color would look good in a room facing East.

"Where were you?" Aunt Minerva asked.

I knew where my brother had been, but Aunt Minerva must have thought the earth had staggered on its axis for Darwin to not be at his post at eight o'clock on the nose.

"Police station," he said without further explanation.

I sighed. It was going to be my job to explain.

Aunt Minerva already had one hand over her heart, the glossy book in front of her forgotten. "Are you a suspect?" she gasped.

Darwin paused, his hand over a silver lever, but he didn't even spare a look for our aunt.

"Computer system," I said. "He's their tech guy, remember? He installed the network there last year."

"Not exactly a network," Darwin grumbled. "Basically two laptops that talk to each other sometimes."

"Either way," I said, "Darwin was asked by Chief Parker to come over and install updates, so he went early this morning while it was quiet."

Aunt Minerva hoisted herself off her stool and invaded Darwin's personal space. She brushed elbows with him and I admired him for not being rude and stepping away. It took effort. I could see that in the stiffness of his shoulders.

"Was it actually quiet over there, or was there a lineup of locals in handcuffs?"

"No," he said.

"Not quiet or no locals?"

"It was a lot quieter than it is here," Darwin said. "No handcuffs. Nobody around at all."

The way he said the last sentence made it sound as if he was imagining heaven.

My aunt gave up the field and headed for the front door. I'm sure she was disappointed that we weren't more involved and informative, but as the excellent woman who raised us, she had to be glad we also weren't implicated in a sensational murder. I hoped.

"Irene asked you to come over," Darwin said just before Aunt Minerva got out of earshot.

"The mayor's wife?" our aunt breathed. "Wants to see Millie?"

"About paint," I said. I glanced at Darwin. "Right?"

He shrugged. "She didn't say."

And of course he didn't ask.

"We've been going back and forth about her laundry room," I explained to my aunt. "She thinks her dryer is a slightly different shade of eggshell than her washer and it throws off the whole room. She thinks I can fix this with the right shade on the walls."

"Easier to repaint the dryer," Darwin grumbled. I thought he had a good point, but no one thinks of repainting their appliances.

"You have to go right over," Aunt Minerva said. "Maybe she'll want to talk about the case."

I sighed and picked up a thick stack of paint samples connected with a plastic rod at one end. When fanned out, it represented nearly every color imaginable. I looked forward to the new ones arriving from the paint company twice a year as if it were a bi-annual Christmas present.

"I might as well go visit," I said. "I can't seem to get anything done here with all my visitors."

"You'd think people would respect your time," my aunt said as she slipped through the front door into the sunshine.

My shop, like the others along Atlantic Avenue, was built during a town revival a hundred years ago. The wide plate-glass windows in vogue at the time had survived hurricanes and Florida heat, and they gave the town an old-fashioned appeal. People who believed Champagne Shores should embrace its potential as a tourist mecca were probably right, even though I wouldn't want to see the charm of downtown altered. The mega-hotels parked on the beach sparked outrage among the residents and business owners downtown until the visitors in those hotels began filling the tables at local restaurants and shopping at stores. Their tax dollars also paid to reconstruct the drainage system downtown and the city parking lot.

Wide glass windows weren't the only thing the True Colors Paint Store had in common with other merchants. I also had a high ceiling with original stamped tin, a tile floor bearing the name of a store that had existed long ago, and antique ceiling fans that still revolved and pushed around the heat.

I loved the paint store with its history, quaintness, and displays of lush colors, but I also enjoyed visiting homes and consulting. It was nice to see where my paint would go, and I almost always got invited back to see the finished project and take pictures for my website. If I didn't get invited back, it usually made me wonder what happened. Did they hate the color and go to a nearby town to get something different and paint over it?

I guess you never really know what goes on behind closed doors.

Mayor Bell's home was a short walk from downtown, and I was happy not to meet anyone asking my opinion about murder suspects on the way. One of the historic homes leftover from a gracious time in Champagne Shores' history, the Bell residence had gingerbread trim, a wrap-around porch, and even a turret. When I was a child, I would walk past houses like this and imagine that the people who lived in them must be very beautiful, too. That was before I realized that people don't always match their houses and that looks can be very deceiving.

I rang the bell and Irene answered right away as if she was expecting me. "Come in, dear," she said. "I have the air conditioning on and I'm still a hot mess. I wouldn't have turned it on this early in the year, but Maurice was just awash with sweat when he came in last night after washing his golf cart. He loves that thing."

A twinge of guilt hit me when I realized he was probably washing off the mud Sunshine dragged into the cart. Yesterday was a tough day for everyone.

"How's he taking Ransom's death?" I asked as we went through the front entrance hall. It was painted a tasteful shade of blue and decorated with family photographs. I'd walked past the wall portraits of their twin daughters my age a dozen times. A long narrow table had older photographs, some with their colors faded and some black and white.

Irene waved a hand. "I don't even know what to say

about any of that business. That man was both a blessing and curse for this town, and now, what a mess. With the annual festival coming up this weekend, I don't know how we'll pull everyone back together."

I nodded sympathetically.

"You've heard people are accusing each other left and right, haven't you?" she said. "Anyone who ever argued with Ransom is a suspect in the eye of public opinion. I even heard you had a spat with him on Saturday morning right in the street."

My mouth dropped open. "No," I said. "I wasn't arguing, I was just letting him know that I'd be a good choice for a paint supplier even if his fancy interior decorator might not think so. Anyway," I said, accepting a glass of iced tea from Irene, "it doesn't matter now that Ransom's dead. As far as we know, the whole project could be defunct."

"I hope not," Irene Bell said. "We can't have a half-finished development."

"Maybe the nephew?" I ventured, hoping Irene might know something about the mystery man so his appearance wouldn't be a total surprise.

"All I know about him is that he's supposedly the sole heir," Irene said. "If you ask me, that makes him suspicious because I don't see how anyone else truly benefits from Ransom's death."

"We'll have to wait and see," I said. I didn't want to ask any more questions and risk upsetting Irene. She had always been nice to my family and supportive of my business and my sister's. "In the meantime, let's take a look at your laundry room. I brought my portfolio with me, and this morning's light is perfect for choosing something you'll love."

"A GIRL'S GOT to eat," Tiffany said, "and it's not casserole night with Aunt Minerva, so we should grab a table at the brewpub."

"You just want to hear the gossip," I said.

"Please. Do you think I haven't heard it all already in my shop? I could write a book. I'm hoping for an upgrade on the gossip by getting a glimpse of the real deal."

"Real deal? You mean maybe watching someone get cuffed and hauled out of the brewpub while the appetizers are still hot?" I asked.

"I mean the nephew. If he's really getting into town today, and he wants to get a feel for Champagne Shores, he'll eat at the best local place," she said. "Right? I wonder how many millions Ransom had."

"I think the nephew is more likely to stay in one of the new hotels and eat there. And maybe Ransom didn't have millions. Aren't rich people usually in debt up to their armpits?" I asked.

"I hope they are at least tall armpits and he's wildly attractive," Tiffany said. "The nephew, I mean. For your sake, of course, since Aunt Minerva said she'd talked you into taking a personal interest in the investigation and then you'd dashed right over to the mayor's house." Tiffany took my arm and hauled me onto Atlantic Avenue. I locked the door of my paint store and resigned myself to an evening of uncomfortable looks, whispers, and perhaps hostility between and among town residents.

Maybe we'd get lucky and it would be casserole night at the homes of the chief suspects.

"I heard Mark Prince was going to be at the brewpub tonight," Tiffany said.

Great. The head of the homeowners' association who had gone to the mat with the murder victim at least a dozen times. Their arguments had taken place in the coffee shop, drugstore, town council meetings, in letters in the small local paper, and once—quite notoriously—in line for the ice cream truck on an unseasonably warm winter day at the beach. Eyewitnesses didn't all agree on who swung an ice cream cone first, but both men had cleared out right afterward and gone home to change.

Mark Prince represented the homeowners on the other side of the development who would be practically cut off by the new community. Recent rumors about Ransom potentially annexing another street of houses and encroaching farther into the southern part of Champagne Shores had reignited passions against the developer, especially when the beach access for the Champagne Circle Homeowner's Association had been purchased by Ransom Heyward. The people of that association, led by Mark Prince, hated Ransom. But enough to kill him?

"He told Hazel he was going to show his face in public just to prove he's got nothing to hide," Tiffany said as we walked the short distance to the brewpub. "She told him he ought to buy a beer for the local police if any of them showed up to dinner, but I thought that might be going a little too far."

"You're right," I said. "He could offer to split a dessert, but booze is too pushy."

As my sister and I entered the packed restaurant, I thought about Mark Prince's strategy of proving he wasn't hiding. I'd had quite a few paint customers who chose colors based on something they wanted to prove or disprove. One man had been accused by his wife of being too timid, so he took her challenge and painted the exterior of his house three gaudy shades of purple. I'd admired his tenacity and his work ethic, painting night and day to get it all done before his wife got home from a trip to visit her mother in Tennessee. However, my heart went out to that poor house that surely didn't want to be a pawn in the marriage game and didn't want to be purple, either.

If we ran into Mark Prince, I hoped to get a chance to talk with him to determine if he was being unfairly vilified or if he had a bit of a purple house painter inside him.

We snagged a booth that commanded a view of the door and the bar, and Tiffany texted Darwin to ask if he wanted to join us.

"He's probably on social overload," I said. "My shop was full of gossip-mongers and Aunt Minerva stopped by three times."

"I'll send him a picture of the specials. We'll see if the pot roast lures him out," Tiffany said.

We kept an eye on the door, watching, in theory, for our brother but in reality wondering if Mark Prince would really show up and make a show of innocence. It should have been a great comfort to him that he was only one link in the chain of suspects that also included the vocal and disgruntled band of motel owners. That group had specialized in competing with each other and giving each other the side-eye whenever they met on the street. They hated each other until Ransom Heyward came along and united them all by providing a common enemy. I knew they still didn't like each other, but the six owners of the small motels previously existing in town hated Ransom more than they distrusted one other.

Reports of angry phone calls, letters, and public spats had fueled speculation that the motel owners would be very happy to have Ransom run out of Champagne Shores. Months earlier, there had been a case of vandalism—attributed informally and without proof to the hotel owners—involving two portable outhouses being found on a barge in the development's recently-filled pond. The prank could have been a whole lot worse, and now the creepy tie-in to the victim being found in that very pond made suspicion of the hotel owners resurface all over again.

Darwin came through the door, cast a quick glance around, and headed our way quickly. He probably wanted Tiffany to stop waving enthusiastically and drawing attention to the three of us.

"There was shouting outside," he said as he slid in next to me in the booth. I don't talk with my hands as much as my sister does and I'm less likely to knock over a drink on him, so Darwin chooses to sit with me as the lesser of two elbowers.

"Who?" I asked.

"Mark Prince and the mayor," Darwin said, reaching for the menu as if there weren't a murder and a showdown looming over Champagne Shores.

I scooted into him and nearly knocked him out of the booth, ensuring that he would never choose me as his booth-mate again. Tiffany was ahead of us both on the way to the door.

When we stepped outside into the mellow evening sun, Mark Prince was indeed arguing with Mayor Bell. The mayor was in the driver's seat of his golf cart parked right in front of the restaurant, and Prince stood in front of him.

"You're full of crap," Prince said. "You're just going to assume I'm glad to see a guy dead because I disagreed with him? Why don't you just go ahead and call me a murderer to my face?"

Mark Prince cracked his knuckles and the mayor set the brake on his golf cart and pulled out the key. It looked to me as if it was getting serious. A crowd formed on the sidewalk, diners who were willing to step away from craft beer and delightfully greasy bar food in the hopes of a great show.

"You weren't kidding," Tiffany whispered to Darwin.

"Do I ever?"

"We should stop them before one of them says or does something he'll regret," I said. I was embarrassed for both of them, exposing themselves in front of a town that was already feasting on the gossip buffet. This was going to make it so much worse.

"No way," Tiffany said. "Let it get interesting first."

"So you went to bed crying last night because Ransom Heyward was found clubbed and floating in his own pond," the mayor said, stepping out of the golf cart. Maurice Bell was somewhere in his mid-fifties and physically fit in a Florida-golfer kind of way. Mark Prince had six inches on him and was twenty years younger. He moved as if he'd played some team sports in his time and had a healthy sense of his own physical superiority.

I would bet on Mark Prince if the verbal fight turned into dueling fists. The crowd around me waited silently, holding its collective breath and hoping for a fight in the same way they hoped for the Gators to go to the Rose Bowl.

"Stop," I said, stepping forward. "No one is accusing you of murder, Mark."

The crowd's eyes swung toward me as if all fifteen people shared one single head. Even Darwin and Tiffany were in sync with the mob.

"Sure as heck feels like it," Mark said. "This clown pulled up here and wanted to know first thing how I felt about my nemesis floating belly-up."

"Did he really say nemesis?" I asked. My other question was *did you really just call the mayor a clown*, but I went with the safer one.

Mark stared at me for a second and then scrubbed a hand through his hair in an exasperated gesture. His arm muscles flexed with the movement, and I was glad for the mayor's sake that no one was going to take a swing. Not tonight anyway.

"It's just such a super villain movie word," I explained. "This is a small town."

I heard someone in the crowd laugh, and I knew I was at least being a sideshow and at best diffusing the tense situation. Chief Parker cruised up in his police car and rolled down the window.

"Everything okay?" he asked.

No one said anything. Soft music poured through the open door of the brewpub, a seagull swooped down and stole a fry from someone who had brought his plate outside with him, and yet we all held our breath.

We heard the police chief's car clunk into parking gear and he took off his seat belt. The action seemed to jar the mayor into movement. "Nothing happening, Carl. I was just expressing my condolences to Mark Prince here for losing an acquaintance like the rest of us."

Mark Prince grunted and crossed his arms over his chest.

"Go have dinner," the chief said. "All of you. And leave the investigation to my...uh...to me."

Even the chief wasn't going to pretend his officers were helping.

Mayor Bell drove off and I watched him turn down the street that led to his house. His sweet wife Irene probably had meatloaf waiting for him, and I was glad for her sake he wasn't showing up to dinner with a black eye. Had he really confronted Mark Prince? Maybe his loyalty to Ransom Heyward was stronger than I'd known.

Mark Prince stalked off toward the grocery store parking lot. Had he innocently shown up downtown for dinner and gotten sidetracked by the mayor? Wouldn't he have brought his wife if he'd intended to eat at the Brewpub? I'd hand over my favorite paintbrush to hear what Prince had to say about the murder. The association he represented had a retired kindergarten teacher in charge of it when I was younger, and it had been a community with no rules. Houses were all different colors, cars and boats parked at random, and Christmas lights were sometimes left up until Valentine's Day.

I used to love riding my bike through that neighborhood where the homes were pretty and colorful. When Mark took over along with a group of young executive types, the streets and homes slowly snapped to attention and fell into line. It only took a few years and the houses took on a uniformity in a palette of only three colors. There were no more campers and boats in driveways, and Christmas decorations were gone by the first week of January.

I missed the old days, but home values skyrocketed and people seemed to like the formal living style. When Ransom Heyward threatened to annex a street on the edge of the association and use it as a wedge to basically cut off the older houses from downtown and—more importantly—beach access, residents of Champagne Circle turned ugly.

In one notorious protest, they'd all gotten their boats and RVs out of the storage facility and parked them in front of the planned development so construction trucks couldn't get in. It was petty and non-destructive, and it was a whopper of a demonstration on how many toys those people owned.

"It almost seems personal," Tiffany said when we'd regained our booth and picked up our menus. Darwin asked the waitress for a fresh drink after he eyed his glass suspiciously. A fly could have landed on the rim or, worse yet, someone walking by could have taken a big swig of his soda. Either one would paralyze him with uncertainty about his beverage safety.

"Obviously," I said. "I thought they were going full fisticuffs."

"Not that. I mean Mark Prince's hatred for Ransom Heyward. I know he was representing the group and the whole boat and camper thing was almost funny, but I saw them argue once right downtown and I thought Mark looked as if he could kill."

"Ransom argued with everyone," I said.

"He didn't seem to take anyone's feelings into account," Darwin said. "No wonder people found him irritating."

Tiffany and I exchanged a glance and we both stifled our grins and comments.

"Agreed," I said. "Ransom annoyed me, too, but not enough for me to want to bump him off. I wonder what caused the final fight that turned deadly? Assuming it was a fight that turned deadly and not a sneak attack or premeditated murder."

"I hadn't thought of that. Maybe it wasn't planned," Tiffany said.

Darwin put his menu down and looked at Tiffany as if she didn't know the first thing about offing someone. "Of course it wasn't planned. Who plans to club someone and shove them in a pond? There are far easier ways to murder a person."

"How much have you thought about this?" I asked.

"Doesn't take a genius," he said. "It would be easy to hide in his house and shoot him. Poison his food or water. Put a venomous snake in his bed. Simple."

"I think I like the Darwin who sticks to numbers and science better," Tiffany said.

Darwin shrugged.

"Assuming the crime was not premeditated, what kind of an argument turns deadly?" I asked. Since the previous morning, I'd tried very hard not to let myself get involved in the investigation and I'd been busy deflecting gossip like I had a nonstick coating. However, the uglier my fellow residents of Champagne Shores got, the more I felt I owed Ransom Heyward a scrap of friendship by at least nosing around into who might have killed him.

He wouldn't have done it for me, especially if I died wearing the hideous apron he thought did nothing for me, but death has a way of eliciting forgiveness fast. Maybe he had simply been misunderstood.

"Money," Tiffany said. "The great divider."

"Women," Darwin said.

On that note, I ordered the steak sandwich special and a gratuitously large beer.

FOUR

HAZEL HAYES LEANED out the front door of her bakery on Wednesday morning, waved like a lost kid in a theme park, and motioned me over before my shop opened for the day. When I walked into her store, I recognized the situation right away. Hazel was staring at the walls as if they had a mind of their own, hand on chin, head cocked.

I approached the bakery counter, and she confessed her decision to paint the walls pink, spilling it like it was a long-held secret. I immediately shook my head. "This room does not want to be pink. Not any shade of pink."

Three tourists sat at a table and Lila who worked at the convenience store perused the baked goods selection.

"You're on the east side of the street," I said as if it was at least the preamble to a good explanation. "You don't get the morning sun through those windows." I pointed at her glass windows. "Evening sun. And that turns pink walls a weird salmon-that's-been-sitting-out color."

Hazel's shoulders sank. "Coffee and a cinnamon roll?"

"Yes to both. Unless you're talking about paint colors," I said.

As she poured me a cup and slid a cinnamon roll onto

a plate, Hazel paused and shot a glance at her back wall. "Yellow?" she asked.

I shook my head. "Not appetizing with this lighting."

"Help me out," she said. "I'm paralyzed by paint."

I took a bite of the sweet delicious cinnamon roll while she rang up Lila's order. The buttercream icing had a hint of maple flavoring, just enough to make me forget it had calories. I washed it down with a swig of hot fresh coffee.

"The answer is staring you right in the face," I said.

"It is?" She looked hopeful, and I relished my role as paint advisor. What would happen to my friends and fellow community members if I didn't help them make wise selections?

"Your shop's name. Hazel's Front Porch Bakery."

Hazel bit her lip.

I sighed. "The tin ceiling wants to be sky blue and the walls are craving a creamy white. Your customers will feel as if they're sitting on a front porch. Those colors take on the hues of the sunrise and sunset without getting tainted and icky. They've been proven on porches all over the South."

"Oooh," Hazel said, her worry lines disappearing. "You're right. I can decorate with a porch theme with wreaths and lanterns, maybe even a wicker chair by the window."

I nodded. "Great idea."

"Can I come over and pick out paint this afternoon?"

"Of course. I have some great ideas already."

The door opened and Mark Prince walked in. He wore a suit and his car was visible through the wide glass windows at the front of the shop. When he saw me, he paused midstride and then recovered and went to the long cabinet filled with baked goods.

"Your coffee and roll are on the house," Hazel said. "Thanks for the paint consultation."

"Happy to help," I said. I should have taken the opportunity to make a graceful exit, but I sat down at an empty table near the register and ate my cinnamon roll. I told myself I was doing it for Darwin's sake because it would be rude for me to waltz into my paint store with a half-eaten roll and nothing for him, but I was lying to myself. I'd never go back to my store empty-handed. My brother and I were operating with completely different types of intelligence, but we agreed on pastries.

"How are things?" Hazel asked Mark with her usual cheer. I was glad I had food I could chew quietly so no crunching would interfere with my eavesdropping. He didn't look happy, but I also couldn't hope for a murder confession over the macadamia rolls.

"I think you can guess," he said. "This is to go."

His business suit and car out front were clear enough indicators that he was on his way to work. I knew what most people in Champagne Shores did for a living, especially those whose skills helped them gain status in the community. One of Mark's selling points for being the leader of the Champagne Circle housing association was his job as a mortgage lender in Jacksonville. He assured people he knew how to raise their property values, and they trusted him with the president's job. So far, he hadn't disappointed his neighbors.

I assumed Mark would grab his food and breeze out the front door as fast as he could, but he paused in front of my table and I looked up. "It was nice of you to…you know…try to intervene last night in front of the brewpub."

Maybe Mark wasn't so unapproachable.

"The special was pot roast, so I didn't have anything to lose," I said. "Besides, I didn't want the mayor to run you over with his cart."

Mark frowned. "You didn't really think he would, did you?"

"I don't know. I thought you were just as likely to clean his clock, for what it's worth."

He shook his head. "This town has gone nuts. Suddenly everyone is a violent criminal just because one guy gets what he deserved."

The tourists stopped chattering and gave Mark their full attention. Hazel rushed over and refilled the tourists' coffee cups while giving them the weather and beach report to distract them. Everyone in Champagne Shores was agog over the murder, but no one wanted our tourist trade to suffer because of it. If we were lucky, people visiting our beautiful beach hadn't read yesterday's *Florida Times-Union* paper out of Jacksonville which carried a picture and a lengthy article about the murder. Matt Riley had a nice byline, and I pictured him writing away in his peach-painted home office. Poor guy.

"No one deserves to be knocked in the head and tossed in a pond," I said.

"I didn't mean it like that."

I took a long slow drink of my coffee. "Okay."

Mark shifted his hot cup of coffee to his other hand and tucked his pastry bag under his arm. "I wasn't the only person in town who Heyward had made an enemy of, you know."

I nodded.

"I could give you a nice long list," he added.

"Maybe you should give that to the police," I suggested. "It's their business."

"It sounds like you're making it your business by nosing around," he said.

I smiled pleasantly, hoping to deflect his accusation that had absolutely no truth. I was not nosing around, and I had no intention of making it my business. I blamed my Aunt Minerva for subtly pushing me into the limelight. And maybe my own curiosity and sense of justice for getting involved at the restaurant. Okay, maybe I was just a shade involved.

"I advise people on paint colors," I said. "That's my superpower. If you're thinking of revising the palette for Champagne Circle, I'd be glad to come out and give you some suggestions. I consult on interiors, too. I could help you and your wife anytime she might want a change—"

"My wife is perfectly happy," he snapped.

The way he said it made me think we weren't talking about the color of the powder room or the entryway.

"Your house is one of the closest to Ransom's development," I said. "I wonder if you might have heard anything Sunday night. Like a fight, a vehicle—"

"A splash?" he asked with a twisted smile. "If I'd heard anything, I would already have told the police."

"Have they questioned you?" I couldn't believe I was interrogating the guy on his way to work. He was just as likely to be innocent as a dozen other people in town, and I was hanging him out in the sun to dry before he'd even had coffee. As soon as I got the chance, I was going to stuff cotton in my ears and barricade myself behind the paint counter with beautiful, safe paint. It covers up ugliness and mistakes, and it doesn't pretend to be doing otherwise.

"You need to mind your own business," he growled and then stalked out of the store.

Hazel's eyes were huge when I turned to look at her. "Scary," she said.

"Maybe he just feels defensive because people are pointing fingers at him."

"If that's the case, Herb and the other motel owners ought to be grouchy, too," Hazel commented.

I sighed and finished off my cinnamon roll. "Too complicated," I said. "I'm staying out of it."

With every intention of minding my own paintbrushes, I went back to my store and tried to engage in the serious art of earning a living. Darwin was occupied with his complicated algorithm of moving cans of stock around on the shelves and shaking them on a periodic schedule. He seemed to know if a can had been moved forward or backward and where it was in the shaker schedule.

His love of patterns and predictability was right up there with his knowledge of exactly which Windows update his computer was on and those of half the people in Champagne Shores. I considered myself lucky he was willing to work for me when he probably could have made a decent living being the town's official computer nerd or writing programs for giant corporations with deeper pockets than mine.

Aunt Minerva came in at noon with sandwiches for me and Darwin, and I knew she had probably already stopped in and dropped off lunch for Tiffany. When our parents died in an accident when I was six and Tiffany and Darwin were four and two, Aunt Minerva and Uncle Foster had scooped us up and taken us home with them. Uncle Foster worked on the highways and the hard work had taken a toll on his back so he mostly stayed home since his retirement and enjoyed the sunshine in his back yard.

My aunt was not the type to sit around, and even though my siblings and I were employed adults, she still mother-henned us and we loved her for it.

"I heard something very interesting," she whispered even though there was no one else in the paint store. "Your uncle is friends with Stanley who does the mosquito spraying at night, and he said he's noticed some funny things going on."

"Like a murder?" I asked, grinning.

"He didn't see that. But he did say he'd noticed Ransom Heyward's fancy black car cruising the neighborhood of Champagne Circle pretty often, including Sunday night."

She had my attention.

"That was the night Ransom was murdered," I said. "I wonder why he was driving around Champagne Circle?"

Aunt Minerva gave a little eyebrows-up shrug. "It's a good question if you know who to ask."

I thought about who I might ask. My earlier exchange with Mark Prince didn't exactly leave the door open for friendly conversation, but he might be interested to know about this new piece of information. Because he was the president of the association, he might know why Ransom was driving around in the housing development. Late at night and on the night Ransom was murdered.

"Poker game?" I suggested. "Stealing street names to use in his vacation community?"

"Girlfriend," Aunt Minerva said. "Stanley said he saw a woman in the passenger seat, but it was dark and he couldn't say who it was."

This was getting more and more interesting. The murder victim was dating someone who lived in the housing development that had declared itself an enemy of his project. Even more intriguing was the fact that Champagne Circle was made up of family homes. I tried to think of any single women who lived there, but no one came to mind.

Darwin put his sandwich in the microwave we kept in the stock room at the back of the store. I heard its timer go off, but Darwin didn't come back out. I'm sure he decided his lunch was better company than me and my highly curious aunt.

"A date gone wrong?" I suggested.

Aunt Minerva sat in Darwin's computer chair. "Do you think a woman could have killed him?"

"She would have to be a tall woman," I said. I pictured Ransom standing in front of me on the sidewalk the last time I had seen him alive. I'm a fairly tall five-foot-eight, and his nose was eye level in my memory, so he had to be maybe six-foot-two. "Striking a fatal blow to the back of someone's head seems to me like it would take some power."

"Or a whole lot of anger," Aunt Minerva said.

Sunshine laid at my feet, her head on her paws but her eyes on my turkey sandwich. I took a big bite, and then pulled off a small section and gave it to her. I knew Aunt Minerva wouldn't be offended by my feeding a bit of her lovingly prepared lunch to my dog. I'd seen her do the same countless times which explained why their Australian Shepherd was shaped like a barrel with legs.

"If a woman killed him while on some date gone wrong, I wonder how she got home?" I said, remembering the morning I'd found his body. "His car was parked in front of the model home where he was living upstairs."

"A woman angry enough to kill a man could probably walk home," Darwin commented as he came out of the back room. He paused when he saw our aunt in his chair. Aunt Minerva smiled at him, but I knew she knew how much self-control it was taking for Darwin not to ask her to get out of his chair. She'd raised him since he was a toddler, and there were many days I'd thought she deserved a medal for patience. We all knew he was brilliant and special in his own way, but it was tough tiptoeing around his oddities.

"And she may have lived close by if Stanley was right. I wish I had walked over to the other side of the pond where the scuffle took place, according to the police. They said the mud on the edge of the pond was disturbed. A woman's shoes would make different marks than a man's."

"You could go out there," Minerva said, dropping her voice to a whisper again. "It hasn't rained the last two days. Things might look exactly as they did the night of the murder."

"That would be trespassing," I said.

"Who's going to care? No one lives there. The project has come to a complete stop, and there's only one nephew who hasn't even bothered to show up yet."

"It's a murder scene," I protested. "And I have no legitimate reason for snooping around."

"Where is your sense of community spirit?" she asked. "Everything you discover helps the police and the entire town. You can't let everyone down."

"No way," I said. "I am not getting involved."

Aunt Minerva looked at me as if she didn't believe me, and I had to admit I was already wavering and thinking about what I might find if I went looking.

THAT NIGHT, I waited for the long beautiful sunset to finally fade. I was usually sorry to see the color and light leave the sky, but I needed complete darkness. I crept down the stairs so I wouldn't catch Tiffany or Darwin's attention. I didn't want to involve my siblings because it was entirely possible I was making a giant mistake. My bike was inside the back of the paint store where I kept it so spiders wouldn't build condominiums on it overnight. I had a small backpack with a camera, a flashlight, and a phone. My long brown hair was concealed under a dark baseball cap and I wore black yoga pants and a long-sleeved black T-shirt.

I looked every inch the cat burglar, and if the police were patrolling the crime scene, my mug shot was going to be spectacularly cliché. I avoided the main street of town as I pedaled toward Ransom's stalled development. It was a Wednesday night in March and the streets were quiet when I got away from the tourist area. I rode on the edge of the road, hoping no drivers would be distracted and dip off the side. I was also hoping no police cars or residents of Champagne Shores would pass me, recognize me, and start asking questions. I'm creative with color, but not a talented liar. No one in my family is. Tiffany is a great listener, Darwin has wonderful attention to detail and realism, my aunt is excessively curious, and I, somehow, was the one dressed in all black riding my bike to a murder scene to snoop around.

I wasn't surprised that the gates of Ransom's development were open. He had never closed them because there was nothing to hide or steal. Even after the notorious portable bathroom on the barge incident, Ransom had simply left the construction lights on all night for a few nights until things died down. The construction workers secured their own trucks and supplies, and Champagne Shores seemed like the kind of idyllic place where crime shrugged and moved on to the next town.

That perception was tarnished now with an icky-colored smear.

I shivered when I rode past Ransom's sleek black car, still parked where it had been on Monday morning. What would happen to it? Would the nephew get a new ride as part of his inheritance? For all we knew, the mysterious nephew was already independently wealthy and living off caviar and champagne in the south of France.

The pond loomed before me, shimmering in the small amount of light from a crescent moon. Had it been very dark three nights ago? I could ask Darwin if we were in a waxing or waning moon cycle. He'd give me a look of sorrowful disdain at my ignorance, but he'd know. I parked my bike on the blacktop nearest the pond and started lurking around the curving body of water. I kept my flashlight in my hand, but I hesitated to turn it on.

I knew the spot where Sunshine had reached the shoreline with the body, so I went there first. There were some narrow stakes pounded into the grass with yellow crime scene tape stretched across in a half-hearted attempt to dissuade snoopers. I stepped over it and swept my flashlight in a quick arc. *Yep. Just as I remembered it.* There were footprints, dog prints, and a large smooth smear where the body had lain.

I recalled Chief Parker pointing to the far end of the pond as the potential site of the altercation. It wouldn't be hard to find if the junior detectives had also stuck yellow tape to some sticks to mark the location. I crept around the bank of the pond in the darkness. Dew was thick on the grass and I could feel the moisture wicking through the tops of my sneakers and dampening my socks.

What am I doing? The thought echoed in my head like a fire alarm. My aunt had played me like a piano when she suggested I could come out here and satisfy my curiosity about the footprints. I should have resisted. I could be in my apartment watching home improvement shows and critiquing their choices of paint colors. The host on yesterday's show had had the nerve to tell a homeowner that shades of taupe or brown were *so last decade* and she had to go with neutral grays instead. I shook my head at the foolishness of having such rules. Rooms told you what they wanted if you gave them a chance.

I nearly tripped over the yellow caution tape and stopped. I took one surreptitious glance around to make sure I was alone. *God, I hoped I was alone.* If there was a killer still lurking about, I would be an easier target than a wounded gazelle on the savannah.

Satisfied that I was the only person foolish enough to be out here, I swept my flashlight around on the ground. I saw heelprints, some deep and some shallow, on the bank of the pond. The ground there was half mud and half sand in a typical Florida combination. I leaned down, hoping to get a closer look and determine if any of the footprints looked as if they came from a woman's shoe. It was a messy scene, but everything in the mess looked like a man's dress shoes.

I heard a small sound behind me. My body froze but my heart went crazy like a bird trying to peck its way out of an iceberg. I forced my shaking hands to turn off my flashlight even though I knew it was too late. With the light out, I felt braver and turned to see who was there. It could be the police and I was going to have some uncomfortable questions to answer. Worse, it could be the murderer returning to the scene of the crime to wipe out pesky amateurs like me who should be home watching television.

In the darkness, I saw a man. We faced each other in silence, both of us clearly up to no good but neither of us willing to flinch first. How well could he see me? Had he gotten a good look at me—perhaps in profile?— before I turned off my flashlight? If the guy wanted to murder me, he'd had the chance but didn't take it. Maybe he thought I was a killer?

"I'm not dangerous," I said aloud, deciding to remove myself as a threat just in case the guy's adrenaline was trying to decide between fight or flight.

The man grunted and it almost sounded like a sarcastic laugh. Did he seriously think I might be dangerous? I could be wicked with a paintbrush and no doubt my opinions were strong, but aside from climbing an occasional ladder with a gallon of paint in a bucket, I wasn't a physical paragon.

He, on the other hand, was tall and appeared strong

and muscular. He stood with physical confidence and something about him finally rang my bell.

"Mark Prince," I said.

The man stepped backward and I knew I'd scored a direct hit. Would he run away, kill me dead, or denounce me to the local police as a murderer?

"What are you doing here?" I asked, letting curiosity push away my other more sensible reactions.

"I could ask the same thing of you."

"Go ahead. I have nothing to hide," I said.

"Which is why you're here at night dressed like a cat burglar."

He wasn't wrong.

"I could be stealing cats," I said. "Working undercover for Poppy Russell."

I heard him huff out a long breath, and then his outline shifted and I realized he'd turned around and was walking away.

"You can't just leave," I said. Not that there was anything I could do to stop him.

He ignored me and kept walking, so I pulled out my secret weapon.

"Ransom was seen driving around in your neighborhood the night he was murdered," I yelled loudly enough for him to hear every word.

Score.

He turned and walked back toward me, moving so rapidly I doubted my wisdom for the fifteenth time that night. I should have brought Sunshine with me, but I wasn't sure she would know when to keep quiet. *Like I did.*

"How do you know that?" he asked, stopping only three feet from me. There was no point in either of us hiding our identity, so I switched on my flashlight and pointed it at him as if it were a mini defense. He put his hand over the end of it and his palm glowed an eerie pinkish red color I would normally have a name for but not when my heart was trying to climb up my throat.

"I have sources," I said.

"Again," he said. "Why are you snooping around and prying into this case?"

"It seems like information keeps coming to me whether I want it to or not."

"That's hard to believe considering you're here at the scene of the crime."

Cold fear washed over me like a sudden rainstorm. "How did you know this was the scene of the crime?" I didn't think the police had released any information, and I assumed only those of us who were there when the body was discovered knew that the actual fatal blow had taken place across the pond.

He took his hand away from the end of my flashlight and pointed to the yellow tape.

"It doesn't take a genius."

I could breathe again even though my self-esteem might have taken a hit.

"So you're not going to tell me why Ransom was cruising your block on the night he was murdered."

"It wasn't my turn to keep track of him. What he did was his business," he said. He tried to sound dismissive, but it came off as bitter.

"I suppose you have an alibi for the night of the murder," I said. I knew I was overstepping with great giant ostrich steps, but I was already in it up to the damp hems of my yoga pants. I might as well provoke the guy and get something interesting to report to Aunt Minerva in the morning. As sure as bathrooms shouldn't be yellow, Aunt Minerva could be counted on to follow up when she had something on her mind.

"What's your alibi?" he asked.

"I was at home."

"Alone?" he asked.

"I'm asking the questions here." I tried to sound authoritative, but that's hard to do when your only qualification is curiosity.

Mark put his hand over the end of my flashlight again and leaned close. "What are you looking for here at the scene of the crime?"

"Tracks," I said, deciding to show my hand. For all I knew, Mark could be as innocent as I was and was merely there out of the same morbid curiosity. "I heard Ransom had a woman in his car when he was seen on your street, and I wondered if maybe that woman could have killed him."

Mark jerked his hand away so suddenly that my flashlight tumbled into the muddy tableau of footprints. It was still on, illuminating the mess.

"Did you think you would find footprints that looked like a woman's?" he asked. He laughed sarcastically. "The police would have to be morons to overlook evidence like that."

I didn't disagree. I twisted my body to lean into the taped-off area and retrieve my light.

"Did you think any of the footprints did look like a woman's?" Mark asked.

Instead of answering the question, I asked one. "If there were, whose do you think they would be?"

I heard him clear his throat in the darkness and the

sound seemed to travel across the pond. What if we weren't alone?

"At least half the people in Champagne Shores are women," he said. "And some of those women had every reason to hate the guy. Maybe you ought to nose around the hotels this place was going to put out of business."

I switched off my flashlight and tucked it in my backpack as if my interrogation was complete. "That's my next stop," I said, and then I turned and walked away leaving Mark at the murder scene. If he was the killer, I'd handed him plenty of reasons to kill again... but also an opportunity in the solitude and darkness of the empty construction site. If he wasn't the killer, there must be a very interesting reason why he was snooping around there at night.

FIVE

"GUILTY," TIFFANY SAID. "Why else would he be there?"

"I was there," I reminded her. Tiffany, Aunt Minerva, and I were having an early morning chat in my paint store. It wasn't opening time yet, but bright morning sunlight poured in the front windows illuminating the thousands of beautiful paint cards along one of the walls. I looked longingly at the paint colors and wished I was talking about seashell versus sunrise coral instead of who killed Ransom Heyward.

"But you're obviously not the murderer," Tiffany said. "You were at home, I heard your television on Sunday night. I could be your alibi, not that you'll need one."

"You didn't know I snuck out last night and visited the murder scene," I said, "so I'm not sure you'd be a rock-solid witness in my defense."

Tiffany frowned. "You should have invited me to go along. I could have held the flashlight for you or maybe snapped a picture of Mark Prince visiting the scene of the crime."

Aunt Minerva and I both laughed. "You wouldn't have gone," I said. "You hate scary things. Remember that time you got up and ran out of the theater during a scary movie?"

"I was getting popcorn. I was very hungry," she said.

Aunt Minerva put an arm around my shoulders. She

smelled of coffee and cinnamon, probably because of the coffee cake she'd brought. Its delicious crumbly topping that was both sweet and crunchy had come down through her family and it always brought comfort and joy.

"If I'd known the murderer would be lurking about, I would have talked you out of going," she said.

Out of respect for her, I didn't point out that she was the one who talked me *into* making the after-dark mission to gather clues.

"I don't think Mark Prince is the murderer," I said, "but I'm double sure he wasn't telling me the whole truth. When I told him I knew Ransom was in his neighborhood, it literally stopped him in his tracks. He was also really curious about what I was looking for and what I'd found."

"Do you think he knows who the killer is?" Aunt Minerva asked.

"Maybe," I said. "Maybe he has a theory just like I do, or maybe he knows and is trying to protect someone."

"Like one of the other homeowners," Tiffany said. "Maybe one of them went crazy and offed Ransom over the whole annex situation, and Mark is trying to deflect blame and keep one of his neighbors out of the slammer."

"Have you been watching crime shows on television?" Aunt Minerva asked my sister.

I thought about Tiffany's idea. "He did suggest I should look in the direction of the motel owners who hated the victim."

"Out of the blue he just suggested that?" Aunt Minerva said.

"It was when I mentioned Ransom having a woman in his car. Mark said something about women being half the population in town and even half-owners of the older hotels in town. It seemed like an off the cuff remark at the time."

Darwin came in the door at one minute before eight and saw me, Tiffany, and Aunt Minerva gossiping over coffee cake.

"Not again," he said. "I wish the police would solve the murder so we can get back to normal."

"You could try helping them," Tiffany said. "Use your computer magic."

Aunt Minerva cut a fresh slice of coffee cake from the pan and put it on a pristine white plate with a plastic fork she drew directly from a box. She handed it to Darwin who gave her one of his rare smiles, took the cake, and went straight to his computer desk.

"Computers only know what people tell them," he said. "No computer will know who killed Ransom Heyward unless the human who did it inputs the information or direct evidence can be cross-referenced and searched."

Tiffany gave Darwin a side-eye as she cut another piece of cake for herself.

"It's the fourth day since Ransom was murdered."

"Discovered," Darwin corrected.

"And," my aunt continued, unbothered by my brother, "finally, the nephew is in town."

"He is?"

"Arrived late last night and stayed at one of the new hotels. The SunBeam. My girlfriend Kathy's daughter works the night desk, and she said a good-looking man got in around eleven o'clock. Travelling alone, well-dressed, said he was in town on a family matter."

"That doesn't mean it's him," Tiffany said.

"The name on the credit card was Grant Heyward," Aunt Minerva finished triumphantly as if she'd just placed a world-class dessert in front of a baking judge. Darwin typed and clicked madly away on his computer, but Tiffany and I were wide-eyed and interested.

"Wow," I said. "Now this will get even more exciting. I wonder where he's been and what his relationship is like with his uncle."

"I'm sure he'll have questions about the investigation and whether or not the police have any suspects," Tiffany said. "It doesn't look good for them if they haven't made any progress."

"I've seen Chief Parker around town talking to people," I said, feeling a need to defend the poor guy. It was a tough job, and even as a civilian who didn't have to play by the rules, I had failed to name any suspects.

We heard the printer whir into life and Darwin got up from this chair. He took a small stack of papers off the printer and handed them to me without a word.

Grant Heyward's photograph smiled back at me in full color from the first page along with paragraphs of text about him. I held up the paper so my aunt and sister could see it and then I started to read.

"Grant Heyward is best known for his documentary films on environmental topics," I read. The article listed ten different films and their dates, and it appeared to me that Grant was a busy guy producing about four films a year. "He's been all over," I said. "Easter Island, Africa, Italy, Grand Cayman, and many places in the United States and Canada. He did a piece on British Columbia and a series on the impact of tourism in the Grand Canyon and Yosemite National Parks."

"No wonder it took him days to get here," my aunt said. "He could have been anywhere in the world."

The printer came to life again and spit out a page. Darwin didn't look up, so I took the liberty of grabbing the printed document. It was a newspaper article from yesterday's Tallahassee newspaper about a film he was making on Florida's Gulf Coast. I held it up. "He was in Florida. Three hours away."

Tiffany gasped. "Does that mean he could have had something to do with his uncle's murder? I mean since he's the sole beneficiary and all?"

Another article came out of the printer and this time Tiffany picked it up.

"Huh," she said, skimming the article. "Maybe he didn't need his uncle's money. His last film was the highest grossing documentary last year."

My aunt snapped the lid on her baking dish. "Something doesn't add up. He was only a few hours away and he didn't come until last night? And why is he the beneficiary? His parents would be about the same age as Ransom, so why isn't his mom or dad the heir to the family fortune?"

"Well," I said. "If the poor man is brave enough to come out of his hotel room, you should ask him those questions. If he's not too busy making funeral arrangements and mourning the death of his potentially only relative."

"Is Grant Heyward married?" Tiffany asked. We all turned to look at her, even Darwin. "Asking for a friend," she said.

I held up a finger as I perused the biography section

of the page about him. The information was taken from an online source about movies and people associated with them such as actors, producers, directors, writers, musicians and composers. "Nothing about a wife and family," I said. "But it might not be included in a biography about his career achievements and contributions to film making."

We all looked at the printer and waited, expecting Darwin to provide the information again. Nothing happened.

"Sorry," Darwin said.

Aunt Minerva headed for the front door with her empty baking dish. "Look," she said, pointing across the street. A tall handsome man was about to enter Hazel's Front Porch Bakery, and it didn't take a sleuth to figure out he was the man we'd been snooping online about for the past ten minutes. He resembled the picture in the print-out clearly enough for a positive identification.

Tiffany and I stayed far enough back from my big front windows so we couldn't be observed as gawkers from the outside, but we both got a good look before he went into Hazel's bakery.

"I hope he's not a murderer and not married," Tiffany said.

"In that order?" I asked.

"I'd take either one."

I smiled at my sister who continually hoped a handsome stranger would come to town and sweep her off her feet. She'd dated Jerry at the bank and Cliff at the convenience store, but I hadn't heard any talk of wedding bells even considering ringing. At twenty-three, she had time.

"How old is he?" she asked. "Just out of curiosity."

"Twenty-nine," Darwin said. "Didn't you read the article about winning the award for best documentary by a filmmaker under thirty?"

"He's closer to your age," Tiffany said, "so you can have him. Especially if he turns out to be a killer or a soccer dad."

"Or both," I said.

"I think you should ask him some questions," Aunt Minerva said.

"If he comes in here shopping for paint, I can promise you I'll ask him all about his uncle and his long list of enemies who wouldn't mind committing a felony."

"You never disappoint me," my aunt said. "I think I'll take your uncle one of the apple turnover he likes so much," she said. She sailed through the front door and straight across to Hazel's bakery.

AUNT MINERVA STOPPED in to report what she'd discovered at the bakery, but I was busy with a customer so she had to whisper it to Darwin. He repeated it to me after my customer left, but either our aunt had discovered nothing or Darwin didn't believe anything was worth reporting. All he knew was that the man believed to be Grant Heyward had gotten something to eat and drink and then left.

Around mid-morning, Matt Riley from the Jacksonville newspaper called to talk with me about the murder investigation. Even though I told him I knew nothing and couldn't possibly comment on something the police were investigating, he kept me on the phone for ten minutes reliving the morning we'd discovered the body and asking leading questions to get me to reveal something interesting. I rearranged a shelf of colorless paint thinner bottles in order to cleanse my mind and prevent myself from saying anything I might regret.

"Can I take you out to dinner sometime?" Matt asked before giving up his line of questioning.

"I don't think so," I said. "If you need help getting rid of your peach paint problem, you could take some pictures of your house and come in to my store. We're open six days a week."

At lunchtime, Darwin placed an online order and I volunteered to go down the street to Cecil's and pick up takeout from the brewpub. Darwin could watch my store, and Tiffany said she'd have time to eat between a highlight and another lady getting an all-over color if our order was ready on time and I hurried down there.

A woman with two cats on leashes was reading the board with the lunch specials in front of the brewpub when I approached. "The salmon looks good," she said.

"Hello, Poppy," I greeted her cheerfully. "Who are these beauties?"

"Saint Michael and Saint Agatha," she said.

Poppy Russell was affectionately known as the cat lady in Champagne Shores. She had a large brood living inside and outside her home four doors down from the mayor's house. She would babysit cats for anyone heading out of town, take in unexpected litters of kittens, dispense advice, and suggest excellent names as long as it was a saint's name. Poppy wasn't likely to run out of those.

"They were both being persecuted at a shelter in Jacksonville and their days were numbered," she explained. "So I saved them."

"They look happy."

"Don't they? Not all cats are walkers, but these two can really keep up."

Poppy was somewhere between sixty and ninety, always wore red, and had ankles as wide as her smile. I wasn't worried about the saints keeping up with her on her daily rambles around town.

I went into the brewpub and Cecil Brooks was waiting for me with a bag of food. "Saw you talking to Poppy out there," he said. "I'm sure glad she didn't try to come in with her cats. I hate saying no to her, but there are health codes."

"She would understand," I said, handing over cash for our lunches.

"Don't count on it. Last time I told her she had to leave the felines outside, she muttered something about persecution. My wife thought she said prostitution, and you can see how that got confusing at first."

I swallowed and tried to maintain neutrality. "I can see that."

"Anyway, Poppy wasn't in much all last week, and it was alright with me. She was cat-sitting for Mark Prince while he and his wife went on some mysterious trip. They wouldn't tell Poppy where they were going, and it drove the poor old lady crazy."

"That wasn't very nice," I commented.

"Well, she talks a lot to people and animals, so I guess I wouldn't reveal anything personal to her either. You have a nice day," Cecil said as he handed me my receipt.

Back on the sidewalk, I looked up and down the street, hoping for a glimpse of Poppy Russell so I could ask her about her recent cat-sitting job, but she was already out of view. Given her slow pace, I assumed she'd gone into one of the downtown businesses that was cat friendly.

"I heard an interesting fact at Cecil's," I said when I went into my paint store. As I unpacked lunch, I filled in Tiffany and Darwin on my encounter with Poppy and the mysterious trip Mark Prince had gone on with his wife.

"Maybe they met up with Grant Heyward over in Tallahassee and plotted to kill his uncle."

"Is there any evidence supporting that wild idea?" Darwin asked.

"No," Tiffany admitted. "But that's what you two are for. Millie can go slink around and snoop and you can be all cyber-genius and look online for evidence."

"Let's eat first," I said.

Tiffany took her food next door so she could keep an eye on the color incubating on one of her customers, and Darwin and I ate in our usual silence. He was a course-eater, so I knew without looking he would eat every single fry before he touched his sandwich. One thing at a time. I was more of an anything-goes eater, enjoying my food with no plan whatsoever.

It was a quiet afternoon, and I stayed busy refreshing my displays and keeping an eye on the street for a Grant Heyward sighting. I wanted to call Hazel and ask if she'd learned anything about him when he stopped in her coffee shop, but I had timed the guy. He was only in there for two minutes and left with just one cup of coffee. I doubted Hazel had much information, especially since she probably got nervous and either clammed up or babbled. I decided to wait for her to stop in and pick up the paint Darwin had mixed for her after she and I had looked at every combination of sky blue and champagne white in my giant wall of colors.

Around mid-afternoon, the front door opened and Herb and Vera Rivers walked in. The middle-aged couple owned the BeachWave Motel just off downtown. It was a classic old Florida place with twelve rooms stacked on top of twelve others and parking right out front. Their small lobby always had condensation fogging the windows, and the sign advertising Color TV in all the rooms seemed as if it was from another time.

Herb and Vera had inherited the motel from Herb's parents, and they lovingly maintained the painted metal railings, miniature palms in concrete pots, and window air conditioning units. I had never stayed in any of the rooms, but it seemed like a what-you-see-is-what-you-get kind of place and I could use my imagination.

"We're closing the motel," Herb announced.

I heard the paint shaker make a sudden stop and I knew Herb had caught even Darwin's attention with that whopper of an opening line. I'm sure my face showed my surprise and I couldn't think of anything appropriate to say.

"Relax," Herb said. "It's just for a short time. We're… uh…" He glanced toward his wife.

"Refurbishing," she said. Standing next to him, they almost looked like the same person. They wore matching orange polo shirts with the BeachWave logo embroidered on the chest, they both had sandy-colored short hair and about thirty extra pounds. I'd known them my entire life and considered them part of the scenery of Champagne Shores.

"It sounds fancier than remodeling or renovating," Vera continued, "and we're really just freshening up the décor and doing some maintenance. Still, we can claim the place was recently refurbished in the travel booklet put out by the chamber of commerce and on our website."

The paint shaker started up again, and I glanced over and saw the expression Darwin used when he felt he was the long-suffering victim of other people's propensity to talk too much. He maintained the website for the BeachWave Motel. He didn't usually complain to me about his side jobs in technology, but I distinctly remember him rubbing his eyes one night and lamenting the owners' insistence on the color orange.

"That's great," I said, mustering enthusiasm. "The BeachWave will be better than ever. Can I hope you're here to pick out paint?"

"Why else?" Vera asked, smiling indulgently.

"You'd be surprised. I've had people in and out of here for the last several days who have no real interest in paint, but plenty of interest in talking about you know what," I said, lowering my voice on the last three words. Honestly, I felt I'd hit the jackpot when Herb and Vera walked in. Combined with the owners of the other hotels in town, they were ranked toward the top of the suspect list. They were local and had a reputation for being nice, but that was the only advantage they had over the owners of the two corporation-owned hotels on the beach. All the motel owners had gone full-ugly on Ransom Heyward in person and on paper, attacking first by going to council and zoning meetings and then appealing to local sympathy with letters to the editor and an advertising campaign.

No one in town could forget about it no matter how cheerful Herb and Vera's orange polo shirts were.

"I'm already tired of hearing about it," Herb grumbled. "That guy was trouble when he came to town, and now more trouble now that he left it. Good riddance."

The body was on ice at the one funeral home in Champagne Shores, so Ransom Heyward hadn't exactly left town. After the medical examiner finished with the corpse, the funeral home took over until the next of kin made a further arrangement. Now that Grant Heyward was in town, what would he do about a service of some kind? Would the body be sent home… wherever that was?

"I'm still hoping it was an accident," I fibbed, "so we can all stop looking over our shoulders and suspecting people we've known all our lives. Like you," I finished with a warm smile.

Vera scratched a spot on her back and looked uncomfortable, and then she pulled out a paint chip that I immediately recognized as the orange color all twenty-four doors were painted. Was it possible that the interiors of the rooms at the BeachWave were also that color? I almost hated to ask. "Can you match this?" she asked.

Despite my raging curiosity and tendency to get overinvolved in problems that are not my own, I am capable of tact and diplomacy. However, this was a time for brutal honesty.

"I've studied the lodging reviews in those travel books you want to make a splash in," I said. "It's a hobby of mine to look through the pictures to get a sense of palette and taste for travelers. In fact," I added in an attempt to keep Ransom's murder alive in this conversation, "I was going to meet with Ransom Heyward on the morning after he was killed to help him choose the interior and exterior colors for his vacation villas and rentals."

"Oh," Vera said. Her shoulders sagged. "How sad for you that you found the body and you missed out on the paint business." She looked genuinely disappointed on my behalf as she scratched her hair. She seemed sympathetic, but nervous. I worked with the king of nervous habits, so I recognized the signs.

"Well, luckily for me, another great hotel in town is in need of paint." I knew the BeachWave was technically a motel, but I thought it was nicer to dress up the name. "It makes up for the loss and then some. Just tell me what you're going for with the new look."

"We ordered all new bedding," Vera said.

Herb cleared his throat and shifted from one foot to the other.

"Color?" I asked. "Or do you have a picture?"

"Same color and pattern as the old, just new," Vera said.

Sweet sugary tea. Just when they had a chance to update the old place.

"Bedding is quite an investment," I said. "And I can see why you didn't want to take a risk there, but I wonder if you might want to branch out a little with paint colors. It's an inexpensive way to give a place a whole new look, and if you really don't like it, repainting is easy."

"Orange is our signature color," Herb said. "Always has been."

"Of course," I agreed. "Nothing says Florida like orange. My suggestion is that you keep it but use it as an impact color."

I was making stuff up now. Generally I would say

accent color, but I thought the more substantial *impact color* would make a better impression on Herb and Vera. They didn't object, and I took advantage of the situation by leading them to the paint wall, choosing an orange much like their previous one but slightly less obnoxious, and waving it past a range of other colors it would complement.

"Look at that," I said. "See how your favorite color has a greater impact when it's paired with these? Now imagine the doors and walls in this nice sandy color with a pop of orange."

I could see they were considering it. "Think of how the before and after pictures will really shine a light on your refurbishment efforts." This was my final effort, the kill statement.

"She's right," Herb said.

"Would you like me to come over and measure the rooms and doors so I can figure out how many gallons you'll need?" I asked.

"No!" Herb and Vera said at the same time, much more loudly than necessary.

"Too much dust," Vera said.

"Construction zone," Herb said. "I have the receipts from the last time my dad had the place painted when I was a little kid. The rooms are the same size. I'll see how many gallons he got."

"We'll call you," Vera said.

After they left, I turned to Darwin. "Anything about that seem suspicious to you?" I asked.

"They talk too much?" he suggested. "They like orange?"

I knew I was asking the wrong person.

SIX

THAT NIGHT, I was halfway through critiquing the colors the perky historic home specialist had chosen for a renovation on television when my phone rang and showed the police station in the caller ID window.

"Hello?" I said, trying to keep any nervous quiver out of my voice.

"It's Chief Parker, and I need a favor."

A favor sounded much better than *I heard you were trespassing at a crime scene last night and harassing innocent people. You're under arrest.*

"Sure," I said.

"I'm at the police station with Ransom Heyward's nephew Grant, and he'd like to thank you personally for discovering the body and handling it with...uh... sensitivity."

"My dog swam out and dragged it in," I whispered, unsure how loud the chief's phone was or how close by Grant was standing.

"Can you come over to the station?" he asked.

"I'll be there in five minutes."

I considered knocking on Tiffany or Darwin's doors to see if one of them would go along with me, but I didn't have to.

"Where are you going?" Tiffany asked before I got down the hall to the steps. "I heard your door shut, and, after last night's escapade, I'm worried you're sneaking out to search the pond for the murder weapon."

I paused. "I wonder if the police have done that? The bottom of the pond is the logical place for it. I'll have to ask."

"You haven't answered my question," Tiffany said. She crossed her arms, waiting me out.

I blew out a breath. "Fine. I'm going to the police station. Chief Parker called and asked me to come over because Grant Heyward wants to talk to me for some reason."

"The nephew? Did he say why?"

"Not anything believable. Something about thanking me for finding the body. Do you think I should take Sunshine along? I feel bad because I left without her last night, too. She's going to think I don't want her company on my late-night adventures."

"I'll go in and hang out with her while you go to the station. If you're not back in an hour, she and I will come looking."

"Fair enough," I said. "I'm recording the show that's on, so don't spoil it for me and tell me if they went with the cranberry walls or the admiral blue. I want to be surprised."

It was a warm night and a peaceful walk to the station just one block over and down. The front door of the small building was unlocked, so I shoved it open and let myself in. The chief poked his head out of his office and motioned me in.

An outrageously handsome man stood in front of the chief's desk. He was tall with dark hair that was a little too long. His eyes were dark and he was tanned as if he'd been vacationing or working outdoors. His white dress shirt with the sleeves rolled showed off his broad shoulders.

"You must be Millie Silver," he said, extending a hand. "I'm Grant Heyward."

We shook hands and he held mine a little longer than politeness demanded.

"I was hoping you'd bring your dog," he said. "When the chief told me about the discovery, I couldn't believe what I was hearing. Your dog must be very special."

"Sunshine is a classic lab. She'll chase anything in the water and drag it in."

I wished I had been more careful with my words as I struggled to read Grant's expression and attitude. Did he seem grief-stricken about his uncle's death? If so, he hid it well under his smooth, handsome exterior.

"And are you okay?" he asked. "It must have been quite a shock finding my…finding Ransom like that."

"I'm fine," I said. "I'm sorry about your family's loss. I knew your uncle and was looking forward to working with him."

"Thank you," Grant said. His tone didn't convey the gratitude of the bereaved. Instead, his *thank you* could have been delivered to a woman who handed him his change at a drive-thru or a man who did his dry-cleaning.

"Was there something you wanted to ask me? I don't want to take up your time because I'm sure you two have a lot to talk about."

"Would you have a seat and join us?" Chief Parker asked. "We were talking about the murder and putting together the pieces we have so far."

"I'm not a police officer," I said, smiling innocently and waving my hands as if someone had just accused me of being the most accomplished pianist in the south.

Grant sat in one of the chairs across from the chief and put a hand on the other, inviting me to sit.

"I understand you're a businesswoman," he said.

"I own the True Colors Paint Store. I help people avoid the mistake of choosing badly when it comes to color."

"She picked all the colors inside my house," Carl Parker said. "When my wife and I moved to Champagne Shores, we needed a kick start to make our house feel like our own, and Millie here is a genius with color."

"I'm not a genius," I said. "I just listen to the walls."

"And people in town," Grant said.

I stared at him and tried for a neutral expression. Was that an accusation?

"Sorry," he said. "I mean you're a good listener. That's what I heard. People talk to you, and that's why you've been…involved…in seeking out my uncle's murderer. I want you to know I appreciate that," he added.

"I don't want to butt in, but if I hear anything useful, I'll be sure to pass it along to the chief."

I started to get up, but the chief said, "We could use your help with the list of suspects."

This was a dozen kinds of awkward. How was I going to enumerate the long list of locals who had a beef with the dead man in front of his relative and heir?

"I couldn't offer any evidence of anything," I said, "so my opinions would be unfounded and probably off the mark entirely."

"Mark Prince," the chief said.

I felt my cheeks get hot. "When I said off the mark, I didn't mean—"

"He's high on our list because he'd been a vocal opponent of the development, had been known to argue in public with the deceased, and when I asked him casually about his whereabouts on the night of the murder, he told me he didn't have to tell me anything."

"I can see why he's on the list," Grant commented. He turned to me and, for the first time, I saw something like sadness on his face. "Did he really hate my uncle?"

"Maybe not hate. They disagreed on land use."

"Did they ever try to work it out?" Grant asked.

As far as I knew, no one in Champagne Shores had tried to sit down and negotiate differences with Ransom Heyward. He wasn't approachable and made it clear that he didn't care what people thought of him.

"Not that I know of, but of course I don't know if they may have had a private meeting. Your uncle has been here in town since last summer, and it would be hard to believe he didn't have a conversation with his nearest neighbors in the last ten months."

"That would *not* be hard to believe. This might surprise you, but I haven't talked to him in ten years," Grant said.

The chief and I exchanged a glance and I really regretted leaving my dog, my couch, and my vicarious redecorating with the help of my television.

"Not since I changed my major in college from business to film. My uncle declared me a flake and hasn't spoken to me since."

"I'm sorry to hear that."

"You can imagine how shocked I was to learn he'd put me in his will as his heir."

"People in town were surprised, too," I said. "We didn't know Ransom had any family."

"You mean he didn't wear the button around with my high school baseball picture?" Grant said.

The chief laughed and then quickly covered it with a cough.

"It's okay," Grant said. "There really was no love lost between me and him. He's my dad's brother, but my parents haven't communicated with him, either. They still live in Michigan and haven't missed having Ransom's expensive shoes under their table at holidays."

"So why are you here?" I asked, feeling irritated with Grant. If he didn't care at all about Ransom, why was he spending his time in Champagne Shores meeting after hours with the police chief to try to solve the murder? He could have gotten his inheritance either way.

Grant looked taken aback. "He was my uncle."

"And?"

"And someone has to clean up after him," Grant said. His shoulders dropped and he leaned back in his chair. "I can't say I'm surprised to learn he left a trail of enemies behind him. I don't travel in the same circles he does, but our paths have indirectly crossed."

"Are you also in real estate development?" I asked. I wasn't going to admit my family had researched him and speculated about him. Anyone in Champagne Shores with an interest in the murder and an internet connection had probably done the same.

"Movies," he said with a smile.

If I hadn't known better, I'd have believed he was a movie star with his handsome appearance and smooth manners.

"I make documentaries on mostly environmental topics. They're probably only watched by high school kids in science classes, but I hope those kids at least stay awake and maybe even learn something."

"What will you do now?" I asked. It wasn't the most

appropriate question to ask a stranger upon the demise of his rich relative, but his answer would go a long way toward explaining him as a person.

He shrugged. "The same thing I've been doing. I've never needed or wanted my uncle's money, and I don't now." He leaned toward me in his seat. "But that doesn't stop me from wanting to help solve his murder. Tying up his loose ends so I can move on with my life will be a whole lot easier without a cold case hanging over his grave."

If I had harbored any hope that Ransom Heyward was just misunderstood and was actually a kind-hearted but shy man who secretly supported orphanages and animal shelters, my hopes ended with the callous dismissal of his nephew and heir. Grant only wanted to clean up so he could move on.

"So who are the other suspects?" Grant asked, returning to what he obviously considered the business at hand. "Any spurned lovers? Shafted business partners? Old ladies he refused to walk across the street?"

Despite his movie-star smile, Grant Heyward was failing spectacularly to make an impression on me. I didn't care how long he had to waste before he could get back to his own business.

"People in this town are tearing each other apart to point fingers," Chief Parker said. He uncapped a dry erase marker and stood at a giant whiteboard on the wall beside his desk. "We need to figure this out before the battle of Champagne Shores makes it into the history books."

If I was going to help Chief Parker solve the crime, it wasn't for Grant Heyward's sake. I was doing it for the people of my hometown, most of whom I'd liked a lot until three days ago.

"Three groups," I said. "We'll start big and narrow it down. Group one is the homeowners who believed they were being cut off from downtown, and an annex in the works was going to make it worse. They were also furious about losing their beach access."

Chief Parker wrote Champagne Circle Homeowners at the top of a large column. "Do you want to fill in names?"

"Not yet. Hotel owners are next." I turned to Grant Heyward. "There are two big chain hotels on the beach, the SunStar and the SunBeam, one of which you're staying in."

"How did you know that?" he asked, a slight grin replacing his look of concentration.

"Everyone knows everything in a small town," I said.

"Well then I'd think someone would know who killed my uncle."

"Someone does," the chief commented.

I wanted to get home in time to watch my recorded episode on television, so I forged ahead. "The six owners of the small motels and possibly the two big hotels in town are the next group because they felt threatened by the competition from King's Ransom."

I paused while the chief wrote Hotels/Motels at the top of the next column on his whiteboard.

"I had an interesting conversation with Herb and Vera Rivers when they came into my store to pick out new paint for the BeachWave Motel."

"Please tell me they're getting rid of that ugly orange," Chief Parker said.

"I think I talked them into it."

"My wife will make you a pie," he said.

"What's the third group?" Grant asked.

"Small businesses in town he refused to patronize or work with. There were no local electricians, contractors, builders, or bankers involved in the project."

"What about you?"

I shrugged. "I was the lucky exception. But it wasn't a done deal. I was meeting him that morning to talk over supplying the interior and exterior paint."

"He liked you," Grant said.

"Only because I was slightly nicer to him than everyone else, and that's not saying much."

"He didn't make a single friend in this town?" Grant asked.

When he put it like that, I felt a wave of sadness for Ransom Heyward. Even his reputed wealth couldn't take the place of having someone to eat dinner with and go for a walk on the beach with. He didn't even have a dog.

"Maybe the mayor," I said, hoping it was at least partially true. "Maurice Bell seemed to be on his side, but it could have been because he saw dollar signs for the city. That's what people in town thought. Most people thought the mayor had his head stuck in the sand—sorry about talking bad about your boss, Chief—because it was obvious Ransom was trying not to benefit anyone but himself. If he'd wanted to help out the town, he would have used local businesses."

"Mayor Bell could have been thinking long term," Grant said. "My uncle's development would eventually have benefited Champagne Shores in tax revenue and residual tourist trade."

"Maybe," I admitted. "Although his development

plans also included its own downtown area with shops and restaurants."

"It sounds like a nice enough place," Grant said. "Not that it matters much now."

I was dying to ask Grant what would happen with the unfinished construction zone currently containing only a pond, perimeter walls, and one model house. However, a sense of decency and sympathy for both Ransom and Grant prevented me from pressing for details on the future of the development, especially since knowing the future wouldn't do anything to change it.

"So we have three big groups," Grant said. "I don't make crime movies, but if I did, I would find it a lot easier to convince audiences someone had a murder motive if that motive was personal." He turned to me, eyes narrowed in concentration. "Who had a personal vendetta against Uncle Ransom?"

I thought about the woman in the car the night he was murdered, but I didn't want to bring it up because I knew so little. Who was she and what was she doing with him?

"You have an idea," Grant said, "I can see it on your face."

I shook my head. "My information is so unreliable I feel that it's irresponsible to say it out loud." I sent Chief Parker a pleading glance.

"No harm in saying it in this room," he said. "We're not a grand jury."

The thought of testifying before a grand jury with any of my hunches or sloppily sourced information made me feel a bit queasy. I had no place playing around in a murder investigation where real lives could be destroyed by accusations and innuendo.

"Just tell us what you know and I'll decide if it needs to go any further," the chief said kindly. "Honestly, I've drawn a big blank. Unless I start charging people and reading them their rights, I'm not likely to find out much more than me and my junior detectives have already found."

I took a deep breath. "My uncle is friends with Stanley who does the mosquito spraying for the town at night."

"I like this story already," Grant said. "Although I'd like to know what chemicals are being sprayed. I did a film documentary on a city in Northern Michigan that was using toxic chemicals that contributed to some serious problems for its residents."

"And Stanley told your uncle he saw something?" Chief Parker prompted.

I nodded. "Stanley was spraying the Champagne Circle neighborhood late on Sunday night and he saw Ransom's black Mercedes on one of the streets."

"Which one?"

"I don't know, but he said it wasn't the first time he's seen that car at night in that neighborhood."

"Maybe my uncle enjoyed going for late night drives? Although I wouldn't do it on the nights Stanley is out there with his bug poison."

"That's not all," I said. "Stanley saw someone in the passenger seat of Ransom's car. A woman."

I let that soak in for a moment as the chief wrote Stanley/car/woman in the homeowner's column on his whiteboard. I felt bad for dragging Stanley into this, and I knew the chief would ask him for details probably tomorrow.

"Who was the woman?" Grant Heyward asked.

I shrugged. "I wish I knew. Stanley said it was too dark and he didn't get a good look."

"But he knew it was a woman?" the chief asked.

"That's what he said. Even if it's too dark to identify someone, I think you can usually tell if the person is a man or a woman." I thought back to the previous night when I'd encountered Mark Prince snooping at the scene of the crime just as I was. I didn't instantly identify him, but I knew my fellow snooper was a man.

We listed names under the columns, working steadily for another half hour. I felt drained and dirty, naming my fellow residents and even some friends as possible murder suspects. Under the homeowner's column, Mark Prince led the list and was followed by five other people who had been outspoken in their dislike of Ransom and his project. The hotel list included the owners of the six small privately owned motels in town, in most cases a husband and wife team. Herb and Vera Rivers were the first owners listed by the chief, and I assumed he remembered the public spats and the bathroom barge incident.

The third column of local businesses was, for me, the most painful. Seeing Hazel Hayes and Cecil Brooks was tough enough. Adding my sister's name and even mine was a punch to the gut.

"Remember not all these people are suspects," the chief said. "Some of them are just people of interest who might know something."

"And be willing to tell," Grant Heyward added.

GRANT AND I left the police station and there was no gracious way for me to avoid walking with him at least as far as my home above my paint store. The streets were quiet. One group of teenage boys skate-boarded past, and there was light and music from Cecil's Brewpub. Farther down the block, the two shiny new chain hotels showed lights in their windows and an outdoor bar on the beach side gave off a glow and a hint of drums from a live band.

The action in town was at the newer hotels, just as it would have been in the new development Ransom had been building. Champagne Shores had to get with the century and offer some excitement downtown or it would fail to attract tourists. Ransom had been right about his assessment of the town and his decision to offer his own inclusive vacation all in one development.

"Can I buy you a drink?" Grant asked as we approached Cecil's.

"Oh," I said, almost choking on the word. "No, thanks. My sister and my dog are waiting up for me."

"It's nine o'clock," he said. "I could buy you a drink and have you safely home before the fairies come out."

I wanted to say no. What would people in town say when they saw me having a drink with the nephew of the murdered man? It would only take one and half witnesses at the bar, and the whole town would know by the end of breakfast tomorrow.

"Or before Stanley gets out there with his truck of mosquito spray," Grant added. He smiled at me as he paused in front of the bar.

He really was handsome. Although I would be skewered by the rod of public opinion, the female half of the town would understand just a little when they laid eyes on the temptation.

"Just one," I said.

As we walked into the pub, I felt as if I were on a date. When was the last official date I'd been on? There had been one polite dinner with a firefighter in town, but we had no sparks. That was a year ago. I'd met a former boyfriend from college at the SunStar's hotel bar for drinks when he was in town around Thanksgiving. He hadn't changed much, and the experience reminded me that I had chosen wisely when I'd bowed out of the relationship and focused on my art study instead.

My formal education about color and design had paid off a lot more than my social life in college. Being with handsome and well-dressed Grant Heyward made me wish I wasn't wearing my after-hours uniform of jeans and a T-shirt. At least my shirt was a flattering shade of pink with the logo and name of my paint store on it. I had also run a brush through my long brown hair before I went to the police station and swiped on some colored lip gloss. I wouldn't win a beauty contest, but I probably wouldn't scare anyone, either.

If the people of Champagne Shores wanted to gossip about me, at least they couldn't say I was throwing myself at the guy. I would have dressed up for that.

"Would you prefer to sit at the bar or a table?" Grant asked.

"Table," I said. "Fewer eavesdroppers."

He pulled out a chair for me and waited for me to sit down first.

"I don't plan to discuss the murder suspects if that makes you feel better," he said. "I just need some company so I don't have to go back to my hotel room and pace the floor until I'm tired enough to sleep."

No matter how attractive he was—or maybe because

of it—I thought discussing a murder was a safer topic than our personal lives.

"So you're traveling alone?"

A waiter dropped off two glasses of water and two menus. I knew every item on the menu, but I picked mine up anyway.

"I'm alone," he said. "I don't have a wife or a girlfriend if that's what you're wondering."

I held the menu in front of my face. "It's none of my business," I said.

"So you have a dog and a sister," he said.

"And a husband and five children." I flicked the menu to the side and grinned at his shocked expression.

"If you cause me to have a heart attack," he said, "people in town will start to suspect you killed my uncle, too."

"Why not?" I said. "Everyone is a suspect."

I placed my drink order with the waiter and Grant asked for the same thing.

"I assume you know best since you're a local," he said.

"Thank you for your confidence," I said, smiling. "Where is your home? The place where you know the best beer to order and all the local gossip?"

"Nowhere," he said. "And everywhere. I grew up in Michigan, but making independent films means you have to go where the stories are."

"You must have been to some interesting places," I said. Although I'd never considered leaving my hometown, I loved imagining the colors of far-off places and dreaming of the frescoed walls in Italy and green hills in Ireland.

"All over. I'm living in a motorhome right now, but I left it on location."

"Where?"

"Other side of Florida. Home base is sort of Tallahassee, but we're doing a film on hurricanes and beach erosion."

"Sounds interesting," I said.

"I thought I was going to make a solid point with the film, but I've only succeeded so far in asking more questions instead of revealing answers."

Our beers arrived and I enjoyed a nice long sip before I resumed my amateur sleuthing.

"Here's a question. If you were just a few hours away when your uncle was murdered, why did it take you several days to get here?"

He looked genuinely surprised. "Was there a hurry?"

"Your uncle was dead."

"Which is why I didn't see a point in hurrying. Had he been clinging to life and anxious to unburden his heart to his nearest relative, geographically anyway, I might have dropped what I was doing. As it was, I thought it was best to finish the filming and give my crew a week's vacation while I came over here to watch the local cops stumble around in the evidence."

"They're not stumbling," I said. "Not Chief Parker anyway."

I took advantage of the break in the conversation and swept a glance around Cecil's. Thursday night beer specials tended to attract a decent crowd, and there were about twenty people in the pub. Three men at the bar, a table with two friends of my aunt's, a table with a couple that looked like they were on a first date, and several other tables with mixed groups of couples and friends.

I could name every person in the bar, and they could all name me and the members of my family. No way was I flying under, over, or beyond anyone's radar.

Grant took a drink and then set his glass on the cardboard circle with the bar's name and logo. "I visited the murder scene this afternoon," he said. "The chief went with me."

He had my full attention back. I scanned his face for signs of emotion. No trembling chin, no watery eyes. Did he really not care?

"I'm sorry you had to do that," I said. I thought about my beloved aunt and uncle. Even if they weren't dear to me as the people who'd raised and loved me and my orphaned siblings, I know I would do anything to get justice if they were ever murdered. Did Grant have deeper feelings for his uncle than he was admitting?

"The chief thought I should see the scene of the crime, but there wasn't much to see. Just some slippery footprints and goofy yellow tape on stakes."

Maybe he wasn't that interested in avenging his uncle's death after all.

"I was much more impressed by the development Ransom had started. It's a nice piece of property, elegant pond, and the model home wasn't bad, either."

I could feel the tips of my ears getting hot as they always did when I was steamed about something. How could Grant speak so callously, and what was I doing having a beer with someone I hardly knew and didn't find all that likable?

"Don't look so shocked," he said. "I feel bad in a general way that a man was unjustly murdered and tossed in his pond, but you have to consider I hardly knew my uncle. I told you I hadn't talked to him in ten years since he disapproved of my choice to go into the arts, not business. But the cleft in the family goes back much farther."

"You don't have to tell me this," I said.

"Why not? I have no secrets." He glanced around the bar as he spoke, and I wondered if he was thinking about the secret someone in Champagne Shores was keeping—at least for now. "My dad and my uncle had an ugly falling out when my mother turned down Ransom's marriage proposal and married my dad instead a year later."

"Wow," I breathed. "That's the kind of thing that leaves a lasting mark."

"It got worse when I was born, and my dad and uncle never spoke again as far as I know. My uncle started to try to contact me when I was a teenager, and we spoke a few times. However, when I was in my second year of college, he came to visit me on campus." He paused and took a drink, and I was torn between not wanting to know what happened and dying of curiosity.

"I had only seen him a few times, and he rolled in driving an expensive car," Grant continued. "I was impressed at first, and I hoped I could heal the family breach. It went well for an hour or so. He thought I was majoring in business which was something he approved of, but then I told him I'd decided to go into film. He looked shocked and I made it worse by explaining that I was interested in social justice and telling the stories of people and places that had been overlooked."

"I think that's an admirable line of work," I said, softening toward him because of the combination of beer and what he was telling me.

"Not what my uncle said. He said he'd thought of me

as the son he should have had with my mother. That was a heck of thing to say to a nineteen-year-old kid."

"That's awful," I said. I couldn't imagine being held accountable for an old grudge.

"And then he disowned me for being soft like my dad and choosing a profession that would ensure I never made any money."

"Ouch." My heart went out to the young Grant who had been treated so unkindly. I was lucky. My aunt and uncle believed in me when I said I wanted to open a paint store. Their only question had been how could they help? My sister chose cosmetology and my brother computers for the same reason I chose art and paint. It was part of me. I dreaded the day my brother, who had finished a bachelor's and a master's degree already at the age of twenty-one, would announce he had a great job lined up elsewhere. He didn't say much, but I loved having his quirky presence in my life and in my shop.

"I let it go," Grant said. "But it was hard to forget. With each successful film I made, my uncle's cruelty started to hurt a whole lot less. Even though it was never about him, I got some satisfaction by proving him wrong."

He finished his beer and I did the same. Now what? Would he offer another? Reopen the conversation about possible murder suspects? Ask me to star in his next film about how paint colors can heal the soul?

"I asked you to join me for just one," he said. "And even though I'm enjoying your company, I try to keep my promises."

I was almost disappointed, but I knew it was for the best. It would be easy to get sucked into Grant's attractive orbit, and I needed to process everything he'd told me. He laid cash on the table that was more than enough to cover two beers and a tip, and I could feel every eye in the place on us as we walked to the door.

"Thank you," I said as we paused in front of my paint store and I dug the key to the door leading upstairs out of my jeans pocket. "It was nice meeting you."

"I'm glad you think so," he said, smiling. "Because I'm afraid you'll have to put up with me until there's a break in the case and I can figure out what to do with my uncle's unfinished business."

As I ascended the steps to my apartment where my sister would be waiting with my dog and a whole lot of questions, it occurred to me that I had started to like Grant Heyward by the end of the night, but there was no telling what the next day would bring.

SEVEN

I KNEW CHAMPAGNE Shores was ready for its second annual festival when I watched the carnival wagons and
food trucks roll in on Friday morning. They went past
my paint store in a colorful parade of primary shades
and bright jewel tones. Those colors would be mistakes
on walls, but they worked on rides and game booths
meant to attract kids with a little spending money. The
food trucks were more interesting to me, and I stood
in my front window to get a preview. Stromboli, pizza,
French waffles, ice cream, smoothies, fried everything,
and an organic beef and dairy offering. I would eat well
for the two-day festival celebrating Champagne Shores
with its beautiful location on the Atlantic Ocean.

I left Darwin in charge of the store and walked down
to the city parking lot by the beach with Sunshine by
my side. Because there were so many out-of-towners on
the festival grounds, I put Sunshine on her leash, just in
case. Watching the food trucks line up where someone
from the organizing committee had spray-painted numbers in the parking lot filled me with a sense of fun and
excitement. It would be nice to think about something
other than Ransom Heyward's murder for a few days. I
hoped everyone in town could come together and make
Champagne Shores look like a great place for a family
vacation instead of looking askance at each other and

wondering where everyone was on Sunday night when the murder took place.

The carnival trucks parked, and the workers began opening the sides and transforming the semi-trailers into rides. Ferris wheel cars emerged, a giant slide took shape, and a miniature roller-coaster track went together piece by piece.

"I'm getting pressure from the mayor to wrap this up." I recognized the chief's voice and turned to find him standing just behind me. He was in uniform, watching the carnival rides and food trucks set up.

"Does that mean you're close to naming a suspect and making an arrest?"

"I wish I were," he said. He rocked back on his heels. "Did you find out anything interesting from the nephew after you left last night? I was hoping he wasn't annoying you and maybe he revealed something useful over a beer at Cecil's."

There was no point in asking how the chief knew I'd had a drink with Grant. Given the gossip chain in this town, it was truly amazing that a man had been murdered and the killer remained a secret.

"I know why he doesn't have an emotional attachment to his uncle and why Ransom left Grant the money instead of his parents. Ransom hated his father for marrying the woman he loved, and he sort of wanted to consider Grant the child he never had. In a creepy way."

"Sheesh," Chief Parker said. "Did anything he said make you think he could possibly have killed off the uncle himself?"

Tiffany had asked me the same question when I repeated my conversation with Grant word for word. On the surface, it seemed possible. He had motive: the inheritance. He had means: he appeared physically capable and he was in the State of Florida when it happened.

"Does he have an alibi?" I asked.

"I was hoping you would know that," the chief said. "I hated to ask."

"He was filming a movie several hours away, living in a motorhome. I'd think someone on his crew would have noticed if he disappeared."

"It's only a three-hour drive and it was a Sunday night," the chief said.

"You don't really think—"

"I keep my options open. He's driving a nice sports car, it's in the hotel lot. It could make the trip fast."

"Have you searched the trunk for a murder weapon?" I asked, sarcasm in my tone. I didn't really think the chief considered Grant a serious suspect even though he appeared to be a good one on the surface.

"I'd need a warrant for that, and I don't think harassing Grant Heyward is what the mayor had in mind when he told me to step up the investigation."

Sunshine laid down in a patch of grass alongside the parking lot and rolled over so the sun could warm her belly.

"Are you going to start bringing suspects in and questioning them?" I asked.

He nodded. "Without a murder weapon or much physical evidence at all, I'm going to have to hope for a confession."

"Tiffany heard something interesting at the salon," I said. "I don't know how this is relevant or even if it is, but she was doing an all-over color on Janet who works part time at the BeachWave Motel's front desk now that she's retired from the phone company."

"Please tell me she found a bloody murder weapon hidden in the linen closet and we can wrap this up," Chief Parker said.

"That would be terrible," I said. "Herb and Vera can't be killers."

"Anyone can be a killer given the right motivation and circumstances."

I thought about that as I watched Sunshine close her eyes and enjoy a sunny nap. Could I be a killer if I had to? To defend someone I loved…maybe. To defend the paint store, not so much. If Herb and Vera had a beef with Ransom, it was business-related, and I couldn't imagine them killing over that.

"Anyway, Janet said the decision to remodel came out of the blue. Suddenly, on Monday morning, Herb announced they were closing for two weeks to remodel and told Janet to go home and take two weeks off. He had a dumpster brought in before lunchtime on Monday."

"Okay," the chief said. He didn't look convinced that this was quality information.

"Janet also told Tiffany that Vera acted very strangely yesterday morning when Janet stopped by to pick up her check. Even though Vera always had the checks ready by Thursday to be deposited on Friday, she didn't have one ready for Janet. Vera told her she would put it in the mail and acted like she wanted to get rid of her as fast as she could. Don't you think that's strange?"

"Remodeling is tough. I remember gutting our kitchen in our former house. It turned our lives inside out for three months, and we fought over the stupidest things," Chief Parker said. He was silent a moment as we watched the carnival workers put together a booth with a big sign advertising ride tickets. "We impounded and searched Ransom's car."

I'd wondered why he hadn't done it right away, but police procedures weren't my area of expertise. "What made you decide to do that now?" I asked.

"Your comment about Stanley seeing a woman in the car on Sunday night."

"Did you find anything helpful?"

"No murder weapon covered in fingerprints," he grumbled. "That would have been too easy. But we did find a hair on the passenger seat. A long blond hair."

I began cataloging all the blond women in Champagne Shores and their hair lengths. Tiffany would be so much better at that than I was.

"We could DNA test it, but there would have to be a match in the system for it to mean anything, and I highly doubt we'd be that lucky," the chief said. "So we put it in evidence for now along with fingerprints we found on the door handle."

"Any chance my sister could look at that hair?" I asked. "No one knows hair and hair color like Tiffany, and she might be able to tell us something about the woman by looking at the hair. She has the only salon in town, and she could probably provide you with a list of anyone in town with hair that matches the found one."

"Anything that will help," he said.

I agreed to bring Tiffany to the station later, and I said goodbye to the chief.

Back at my shop, I recalled my conversation from two days earlier with Vera and Herb Rivers. If they were closing for only two weeks to remodel all twenty-four rooms and repaint them, they needed to get busy. As a courtesy, I had Darwin mix up samples of the sand color and orange color we discussed when they were in my shop. Maybe if I went over there and took them the complimentary samples along with the matching paint cards, it would spur them into action deciding how many gallons they would need. Honestly, if they would just let me measure one room, I could figure an estimate in no time, assuming all the rooms were the same size.

In a perfect world, they would update the lobby area as well because that was first-impression zone for tourists and visitors. If I went over and talked to them, it might be a great help as they beautified their long-standing business. Although I didn't want to admit it when my brother pointedly asked why I was so anxious to help the Rivers', curiosity was part of my motivation. Perhaps I could learn something helpful to the investigation and put all our minds at rest.

When I walked up to the BeachWave Motel, the first thing I saw was a large dumpster in the parking lot. It took up three spaces. The second thing I saw was the police chief's car parked right in front of the hotel's office. Because I was on foot, I could approach the office quietly and without notice, even though I battled the urge to turn around and run away.

What I heard when I got to the open door shocked me. Herb Rivers was shouting at Chief Parker. "You're not searching my hotel, my dumpster, or any other part of my property without a warrant."

I heard the chief calmly asserting that he could get a warrant and be back within a few hours, and it would be far better to cooperate and make it easier on everyone involved. I crept into the lobby and hid behind the counter where I could hear everything but not be seen. My detective skills were pathetically basic but effective.

Herb Rivers used some language that would have shocked my Aunt Minerva and most of the people I knew, and then the chief politely explained that he would return with a warrant and advised Herb not to try to cover anything up or remove anything from the property in the meantime.

I shrank farther into my hiding spot, afraid of getting caught and thrust into the middle of the ugly scene. The chief stalked past, sending a breeze over me, but he didn't see me.

As soon as the chief left, I realized my mistake in staying quiet. Whatever Herb said now, I would be privy to whether I wanted to be or not. I did not want to hear him discussing the murder with his wife, a fact I should have considered before I crept into his lobby and hid under the counter.

"You know what they're going to find when they come back," Vera said, her voice quivering with emotion.

Oh my goodness. Could it be true that Herb and Vera killed Ransom Heyward and tossed evidence in their dumpster? Could the murder weapon be at the bottom of all the construction mess and mattresses?

"It's too late to hide it," Herb said bitterly. "And you know he's going to have someone watching the place. If we try to clean out the dumpster, it'll look even worse for us."

I crept out from under the counter and stood in the doorway. I tapped loudly on the open glass door and yelled, "Hello, anybody here? It's Millie from the paint store."

I hoped they would buy my just-showed-up act, especially if they were killers. Slipping out the door and running away crossed my mind, but I was afraid they would emerge from the office just in time to see me retreating across the parking lot, and that would make me look guilty.

I felt guilty enough already. Wasn't I the one who told the sheriff the story about Herb and Vera closing suddenly and without warning and then acting all weird about their employee's checks? I had brought the police chief to the Rivers', and now it was going to get ugly. Fast.

Vera came out of her office, looking as if she was about to cry.

"I brought samples," I said cheerfully, holding up the two small jars. "Sandcastle and sunset orange. I think you're going to love them!"

Vera swallowed. "Just…just leave them on the counter," she said, her voice a barely audible whisper. "We'll try them out later."

"Sure," I agreed pleasantly as if there wasn't a heavy cloud hanging over the office. "While I'm here, can I just measure up a room so I can calculate how much paint you'll need? I heard you were only closing for two weeks, so I know you can't afford to waste a minute."

"Who said it was two weeks?" Vera asked.

"I…uh…think you told me that yourself when you were in my shop on Wednesday. And Janet was at my sister's place and said something about a two-week vacation while Tiffany was coloring her hair."

"I hate this town," Herb growled from the inner office. I couldn't see him, but his sentiment was clear.

"You should go," Vera said, glancing nervously at the parking lot.

"I know you're busy," I said. "Just let me know if

I can help." I walked as fast as I could across the lot without running. A police car was parked across the street commanding a full view of the hotel office and dumpster. Herb was right about the surveillance, and I realized with cold certainty that the chief wasn't messing around.

"GRANT HEYWARD CAME to see you while you were out," my brother said when I returned to my store. At that moment, I felt genuine compunction for every time I had complained about the slow pace of life in Champagne Shores.

"Did he say what he wanted?" I asked.

"No."

"And you didn't ask?"

"He wasn't here to see me," Darwin said. "He left his number." My brother handed me one of my own business cards on which Grant had written his name and number.

"I think something bad is about to happen at the BeachWave Motel," I said.

Darwin continued mixing paint without taking my bait.

"Maybe an arrest in Ransom's murder case."

"That sounds like a good thing," Darwin said. "People in Champagne Shores will be able to sleep at night and go back to worrying about the weather, their sports teams, and their neighbor's business."

"I feel responsible," I said.

"Did you kill Ransom?"

"Of course not," I said, both hands raised.

"Then—"

"Don't be so literal," I said, snapping at him.

Darwin glanced up and studied me as if I were a code he couldn't break. "Tell me what's happening at the BeachWave. If you have to."

Tiffany opened the front door. "All my appointments are done for the day and I'm putting up a sign that I'm closing. Too bad for any walk-ins. It's Friday, and I heard the festival food wagons are opening for dinner."

She put her purse on the counter and sat on one of my stools.

"Has something happened?" she asked. "You both look serious. Darwin usually does, but you look… unnerved," she said, finding the right word.

I still had the business card in my hand with Grant's phone number on it, and Tiffany's sharp eyes zeroed in on it.

"Is that a phone number?" she asked.

I sighed. "I have a lot to tell you."

Over the next five minutes, I filled Tiffany in on the blond hair found in Ransom's car and what I'd overheard while hiding under the check-in counter at the BeachWave.

"I'd like to see that hair," she said.

"I'm not sure it matters now. Whatever woman was in Ransom's car that night, I doubt she was staying at the BeachWave Motel."

"We could stop by and take a quick look on our way to the food wagons," Tiffany said. "I say you should close your store a few minutes early, and we all make a quick stop at the police station and then hang out at the festival. We need greasy food and some fun."

"What do you say, Darwin?"

"It's four-forty-eight," he said. "We close at five."

Tiffany and I exchanged a glance. "Okay. We'll go

upstairs and change for the festival, and by the time we're ready, it will be five o'clock and we can all go together."

Darwin shrugged. "Okay."

At five after five, all three of us were at the police station. And we weren't alone. Both police cars were out front, and when we entered the station, we heard yelling. The chief's voice was calm and quiet, but Herb Rivers was putting up a verbal fight. I hoped the other two officers were with the chief so he had backup.

"We'll come back another time," I told Gladys who stood by her desk with her purse over her shoulder. She was obviously leaving for the day, and like everyone else in town, probably anxious to get to the festival.

"The chief said you'd be stopping by," she said. "It'll just take you a minute to look at the hair." She waved us into a side office and opened a filing cabinet. We could still hear everything being said next door. Herb was saying it was none of the chief's business where he was on Sunday night when the murder took place. He also added he had no idea how the murder weapon got into the bottom of his dumpster.

Tiffany and Darwin locked eyes with me when we heard him say that.

"I know," Gladys said. "It's a shocker. The chief hadn't even planned to search the dumpster until he visited Herb earlier today and the guy was so cantankerous about it. Seemed like he had something to hide, so the chief got a warrant fast from the judge."

She laid the hair in a sealed plastic bag on the counter in front of Tiffany. "Better look quick," Gladys said. "This evidence might end up going off to the state crime lab along with the murder weapon."

"Are you sure it's the murder weapon?" I whispered, unable to believe Herb or Vera would go that far.

"Chief sure seems to think so," Gladys said in a low voice. "It's a crowbar with something red and sticky on it."

I thought back to Herb's bitter words to Vera earlier in the afternoon about how it was too late to hide something now. If he knew the murder weapon was in his dumpster, wouldn't he have at least tried to dig it out and hide it when he knew the chief was coming back with a warrant?

Tiffany examined the hair and held the clear plastic bag up to the light. I drifted toward the door where I could hear the chief's conversation with Herb more clearly.

"That's none of your business either," Herb said.

For a man accused of murder and whose dumpster was just found to contain a suspected murder weapon, Herb was being incredibly loud and difficult. It seemed to me that cooperation in such a case would be more helpful, but maybe he figured he had nothing to lose.

I overheard the word "lawyer," from Herb, and I knew the interrogation was at an impasse.

"You can cooperate or you can sit in the cell and think about it," I heard the chief say. He was usually a pleasant guy, but his usual duties in Champagne Shores didn't include arresting locals on suspicion of murder.

As I stood in the doorway, Mayor Maurice Bell burst through the front door of the police station. He was flushed and his forehead was damp with sweat.

"I heard there's been an arrest," he said.

I turned to Gladys, hoping she would answer the

question because I was way outside my jurisdiction on all of this.

"The chief is questioning him right now, but it doesn't sound like he's cooperating," Gladys said.

"Well he darn well ought to," the mayor said. "It may be the only thing that keeps him from a lifetime in prison or worse."

I heard Tiffany gasp and even Darwin looked shocked. The five days since the discovery of the murder had been a roller coaster, but now it felt as if the ride was speeding out of control.

"I would say it's a younger woman, but not too young," Tiffany said, looking closely at the hair. I was impressed that she was maintaining her focus when things had taken a wild left turn since we walked into the station. "Maybe twenties or thirties. And she's a natural blonde. This doesn't look treated or colored. Lucky lady," she said.

"What are you talking about?" the mayor asked.

I again looked to Gladys. Even though the mayor was technically in charge of the police department, I didn't know how closely he was involved in evidence collection.

"Hair found in Ransom's car," Gladys said. "Stanley the sprayer reported seeing a woman with him the night he was murdered, and it looks like Stanley was right."

"A blond woman?" the mayor asked.

Tiffany nodded. "Long blond hair, at least shoulder length, maybe longer."

I could see the mayor working that information into his head and turning it over.

"But now that Herb's been arrested, the rest of the investigation is probably over," Gladys said.

"No one said anything about it being over," Chief Parker said. He came out of his office and loomed large in the central hallway lined with pictures of past chiefs and a large map of Champagne Shores. Behind him, we saw the two other police officers lead Herb toward the back of the station in handcuffs.

"He's asked for a lawyer and clammed up," Chief Parker said. "And I don't blame the guy. It's the smartest move he could make now that I've read him his rights and arrested him. As for his innocence or guilt, we've got a long way to go before we get there."

"Good work, chief," the mayor said.

"I had help. Millie supplied some information she overheard and we followed a hunch." He turned to Tiffany. "What did you think of the hair?"

"Wait a minute," the mayor said. "Herb and Vera both have short hair and they're not blondes."

"So?" the chief said.

"So what does it matter about the hair in Ransom's car? You should be focused on evidence supporting your arrest so the good people of Champagne Shores can enjoy the festival."

"They'll enjoy it," Chief Parker said.

"A woman in her twenties or thirties, natural blonde, at least shoulder-length," Tiffany said.

Chief Parker nodded. "If you see anyone at the festival matching that description, start a list," he said.

Tiffany, Darwin, and I left the police station and turned toward the downtown parking lot from which we heard music and laughter and smelled delicious fried food.

"Not sure I feel like partying," I said.

"I know," Tiffany said. "But Aunt Minerva and Uncle

Foster will be there, and I promised we'd see them. Aunt Minerva wants to make sure her beach bag is prominently displayed in the prize package at the city's booth after she hurried to get it done this week."

I laughed. "I'm sure it is."

"I hope so," Darwin muttered. "She made me put it over my shoulder yesterday when she stopped by to make sure it was scaled for a man or a woman."

Tiffany grinned. "Did it fit you?"

"It's a bag," Darwin said. "Bags don't have a fit or a gender preference." He rolled his eyes. "I drew the line at putting my laptop in to see if it would double as a computer bag."

"Now we'll never know," I said.

Tiffany grabbed my arm and pointed. "Look who's here," she said.

Grant Heyward stood at the Stromboli wagon's front window. We watched him point to the sign and then hand over cash. Instead of a dress shirt and pants, he wore a polo, shorts, and sneakers. The man in line to inherit numerous properties and a lot of money looked just like any other tourist as he smiled at the girl running the stand and took the paper plate with his dinner on it.

"You should go say hello," Tiffany said. "What if he doesn't know anyone else in town and has to eat alone?"

As I considered approaching him, Maurice Bell swept out of nowhere with his wife. Mrs. Bell gave Grant a hug and nearly tipped his Stromboli onto her white linen blouse and matching pants. She was such a sweet lady that it would have been a shame. From their animated conversation, it was obvious that the mayor was delivering the big news to Grant about the arrest.

He must have come straight from the station just like we did.

I waited for Grant's reaction, but instead of looking excited or even mildly happy, he nodded seriously as if they were talking about the very best way to get a tomato stain out of white fabric.

"He looks like he would rather be eating that sandwich than hearing about his uncle's murderer being arrested," Tiffany said.

"I can't blame him," I said. "I'd rather be eating, too."

We split up briefly and went to different food wagons to indulge our own personal taste, but we agreed to meet at the picnic tables in a few minutes. I was the last one to get to the table because I'd chosen my food wagon by which one had the longest line operating on the assumption that popularity equals quality. My aunt and uncle were already seated with my brother and sister when I plunked down my gyro and mozzarella sticks.

"Are you happy with how your beach bag turned out?" I asked. "I haven't been to the raffle booth yet, but I know I'll be buying a ticket."

"I ended up loving the stripes," she said. "I don't want to make a habit of waffling on color like that, but it was just the trick for this one."

"What's your next project?" I asked.

It was nice talking about anything other than the murder investigation and the arrest of Herb Rivers. I knew Tiffany had already filled my aunt and uncle in on everything we knew while they waited for me to get to the table, and I was glad to miss it. The entire affair made me feel creepy and sad for Ransom and for Herb. How had things gotten so far out of control?

"I'm making an afghan for April May's sister who just went into senior living," Aunt Minerva said.

"Color?" I asked. I knew my aunt's friend April May who owned the antiques and yarn shop, but I didn't know her sister. April was an interesting lady who loved to tell the story of how unlucky it was that she fell in love with and married a man whose last name was May. I wondered if her sister was also a character. The color my aunt chose for the afghan would tell me everything I needed to know about the recipient.

"Red with an orange border," Aunt Minerva said.

"Is she that bad?" Tiffany asked, her eyes huge.

"From what I hear. She drives poor April nuts and got kicked out of the last senior living apartment for yelling out her window and telling a man to get off her lawn."

"Was he trespassing?" I asked.

"He was with the lawn service," Aunt Minerva said.

Maybe it's a family trait, but my aunt has definite opinions about yarn colors suiting the recipient of the finished item. All baby blankets and gifts are green, and if she really likes the parents, she puts a pretty white frilly edge on the gifts. Yellow gifts are for people she considers complicated but basically good. Blue and purple are favorite colors reserved for people she loves. White is her neutral color, and black items are reserved for people she thinks are negative but without passion. Orange and red are colors for people she considers negative with too much passion, and it sounded as if April's sister was a perfect candidate.

As we ate, I kept my eyes open for Grant Heyward. I probably should have been looking for blond women, but I knew Tiffany would have that covered for the chief. I should have been relieved that a suspect had been arrested and a murder weapon found, but instead I had that unsettled feeling I got when a paint color wasn't right. I'd spent a weekend last summer repainting my bathroom when I switched on the light over the mirror and the blue I'd chosen for the walls reflected my face back to me as if I were a puppet in a children's television show—and not the cute puppet. It was that sort of feeling.

If only a gallon of paint would pretty up the rough week it had been.

EIGHT

DARWIN WENT HOME right after we finished our festival food, and Tiffany went off to talk with a group of her friends from high school. Most of my high school friends had left town to seek love or fortune or both. I didn't regret staying in Champagne Shores and building my paint empire one bucket at a time. Would I ever be a household name and franchise out my True Colors Paint Store to other cities where people were making color mistakes on their interiors and exteriors? I smiled, imagining it as I watched my sister and brother walk away.

I was happy being right where I was.

"You don't have to babysit me," I told my aunt and uncle. "I'm going to take a walk through the rides and then I'll probably head home and put my feet up. The festival might inspire me to dream up some new colors that will drive Darwin bonkers when he tries to mix them based on my description and vision."

"He'll want to know how many parts blue and yellow, and you'll be describing a field of wildflowers," my uncle said, smiling. How well he knew us.

They said goodnight, and I wandered along the strip of carnival rides. With their flashing lights and cheerful music, the rides and booths lit the night and made me feel better about the murder case. I had confidence in Chief Parker. If Herb Rivers, and maybe his wife, too, were guilty of murder, the chief would handle the case professionally. If they were innocently accused, Chief Parker would find out and let them go. Even with my vivid imagination, I couldn't reconcile their conversation about hiding their dumpster contents with the fact that I wanted them to be guiltless in Ransom's murder. Maybe they were hiding bedspreads and lamps so ugly they had the power to kill? I had to have faith that justice would be served either way.

As I walked, I noticed a sandy-haired man ahead of me and instantly recognized him as Matt Riley from the Jacksonville paper. Had he already heard about the arrest of Herb Rivers? There was probably no one at the police station to talk to, so maybe he'd come to the festival hoping to score a conversation or a quote from someone in town. It was also possible he was there for the fried pickles, but I didn't think it was likely.

In true cowardly fashion, I hid behind a tent where the local cheerleaders sold glow necklaces until Matt Riley disappeared. Taking my opportunity, I popped out from behind the tent and decided to make my way home before Matt turned at the other end of the midway and began walking back my direction.

Right in front of me, a scrambler ride whirled and rushed its riders around in a tight circle. Children squealed and parents held up smartphones, trying to capture photos of their fast-moving offspring. My aunt and uncle had taken Darwin, Tiffany, and I to Walt Disney World several times when we were younger, and their attempts to photograph us on spinning tea-cups usually resulted in great pictures of someone else's children.

A tall attractive man, hands in pockets, also watched the ride. He grinned when he saw me.

"Are you thinking of making a documentary on the plight of carnival workers?" I asked.

Grant's grin turned into a full-blown magnetic smile. "I was actually thinking of a film on why street fairs and tacky rides are an important part of the American experience."

"Don't people in other countries also enjoy putting their children on flashy but poorly constructed rides?" I asked.

"And eating food that is so dangerous it could probably be weaponized," he said, laughing. "Yes. I've been to street fairs in Europe, and they're basically like this one. Champagne Shores has the benefit of a seaside location, though."

"Not that you can see the ocean in the dark or hear the waves over the carnival music," I said.

He held out his hand. "If we took a walk on the beach we could."

I hesitated, wondering how involved I should get with Grant. Already, the news about the arrest of Herb Rivers would be spreading from house to house like a wildfire of information. Lines of friendship would be drawn, sides would be taken. Where did I want to be?

"I'd like to hear your thoughts on Herb Rivers," he said, "and I don't want to have to shout above the noise here."

I didn't take his hand, but I did nod my head toward the beach and start walking. It was better than risking an interview with the reporter. Grant followed and we left the lights and atmosphere of the festival. On the edge of the beach, I paused and removed my shoes.

Grant did the same. The sand had cooled when the sun went down, but it still felt wonderful on my feet as it squished between my toes. Living on the beach was one of the many reasons I would never want to leave Champagne Shores.

"The mayor was anxious to tell me the good news," he said as we approached the water's edge. There was no one else on the deserted beach, and Grant must have felt he could speak freely. "He seems to be taking it personally, my uncle's death."

"I think he liked Ransom," I said. "Maurice Bell isn't originally from Champagne Shores, and maybe it helps him take a broader view of the town's future. He was more open-minded about a vacation development and his support pushed the permits through for your uncle's project."

"Did you like the idea of the vacation community?"

"It wasn't popular to say so in town, but I thought it had a lot of merit. Renting a vacation home instead of staying in a hotel seems to be a huge trend. I'm sure it's nicer for families to have more room and a kitchen and all."

"He's been successful with the same concept in six other places," Grant said. "He built a community like this in two Gulf Coast cities in Florida, one on the Carolina Coast, two in Texas, one in Maine, and I think his next conquest was going to be California."

"I thought you weren't close to your uncle and hadn't talked to him in ten years?" I said.

He shrugged. "I followed his career, and it wasn't hard when he tended to go big on advertising and promotion. Calling his vacation homes King's Ransom sort of says it all, doesn't it?"

I laughed. "It does. People in town thought that name was a bit…"

"Narcissistic? Vain? Over the top?"

"Maybe," I agreed. "But it does sell the luxury vacation idea."

I heard Grant sigh. "And now what?" he asked. "What does a cast-off nephew who is not interested in real estate do with an empire he unwittingly inherited?"

Although I was put off by his callous attitude when I first met him in the police station, Grant was rapidly improving in my eyes. He wanted to pick up after his uncle, and the tone of his voice expressed a vulnerability I found slightly endearing. What would he do?

"I have no idea," I said honestly. "I can't imagine."

"Me neither. As you know, my uncle was disappointed because I chose arts over business, and that difference is staring me right in the face now."

"You can get help," I suggested. "Attorneys who specialize in this sort of thing."

"I'm already looking into it. I feel like a fish out of water, an imposter at the royal ball," he said with a half-laugh. "I can't even take this experience and make it into a movie because it's definitely not my brand. I make films about people fighting for access to clean water, people who protect turtles hatching on public beaches, and boats damaging protected reefs in high tourist traffic areas."

"Admirable," I said.

He laughed. "Don't think I'm a saint. To make those films, I get to go on location in Florida, the Atlantic seacoast, beautiful islands, and the Bahamas. If I choose my time of year wisely, I never have to see snow again."

"You don't like cold weather?"

"I hope I shoveled my last driveway and scraped my last windshield when I left Michigan after college."

"Can you believe I've never done either of those things?" I asked. "We do get a frosty morning every now and then in the winter, but I don't drive to work so I just go downstairs and wait for the sun to warm everything up."

"A true Florida girl."

We walked along the edge of the water. The lights of the two corporate hotels were ahead of us and the street fair was behind us.

"It almost seems too good to be true," Grant said. "Murder weapon conveniently found in a dumpster of someone known to detest the victim. The only thing easier would be a confession."

"I don't think that's going to happen," I said. "Herb doesn't appear to be cooperating."

"I guess I wouldn't either if I thought I was facing life in prison for killing a guy," Grant said.

My toes got too close to the water and a cold wave washed over my foot. It seemed like a reminder from the ocean that I was walking on a deserted beach with a guy I hardly knew, and that man had just inherited a fortune because of an untimely death.

"I'm going to take the shortcut home," I said. I pointed straight ahead. "If you follow the beach, you'll be back to your hotel in three minutes."

"Millie, I—"

"Thanks for a nice walk on the beach," I said brightly. "But I have to go. My store opens at eight on Saturday mornings, and it's always a busy day."

I strode across the sand, took only a moment to slide my sandy feet into my shoes, and headed for the comforting strip of shops downtown. With the orderly streets, lights, sidewalks, and familiar names, down-town made sense to me.

Walking along the deserted beach with Grant did not.

"COULD I PERSUADE you to go across the street and get us coffee and rolls?" I asked Darwin on Saturday morning.

He looked up from his computer screen. "Why?"

"Why do I want coffee and rolls?"

"No, why do you want me to go?"

I sighed. "I'm tired of all the drama and gossip. Hazel will want to discuss every detail of the case. She'll have a theory about the murder weapon and how it got into the dumpster at the BeachWave Motel. She'll want to know everything I overhead when I was at the police station because I already know Gladys told people we were there."

"And you think I'll go throw myself on that fire?"

"No," I said. "I think Hazel will just hand you cof-fee and rolls and let you go without rehashing the whole thing."

"Why?"

"Because you have a reputation for being…not a gossiper," I finished. I didn't want to say unfriendly or anti-social because those weren't accurate. Darwin was Darwin. Some days he drove me nuts, and some days I thought we needed a dozen more people just like him in town.

I could see he was considering my request, so I handed him a ten-dollar bill from the cash register. "Get extra icing," I said.

I paced the store, filled with pent-up energy and questions. It wasn't my business to tell the police what to do, and I knew they must have known something I didn't know because, in my mind, the pieces weren't all fitting together. Did the pieces usually fit neatly when a murder occurred? Maybe I would ask Chief Parker if I got the chance.

When Darwin returned from the bakery, I gave him a full minute to put the coffee and rolls down before I pounced.

"Any news?"

He tilted his head. "If you wanted news, why didn't you go?"

"That's beside the point."

"No, it isn't," he said neutrally as he poured his coffee from the white foam cup into his favorite ceramic mug. I wasn't surprised. Darwin had a texture thing.

"Fine, it isn't beside the point and I know I should have just gone if I wanted news…but—"

"Grant Heyward was at a table with a woman I've never seen before," Darwin said.

"What? How did they get in there? I've been watching the front door for ten minutes."

"I assume they've been there longer than ten minutes," Darwin said.

"Who is she?"

"I already told you I've never seen her before."

"And you didn't find out from Hazel or somebody?" I asked.

"You sent me for coffee and rolls. I even got the extra icing. That was my mission."

"Description?" I asked.

"Cinnamon rolls. Black coffee."

"I'm going to murder you," I said. "And toss the weapon in the dumpster at the BeachWave Motel."

Darwin smiled, one of his rare beautiful smiles. "The woman is older than we are but not a lot. Definitely not old. Long blond hair. Blue shirt."

"Girlfriend maybe?"

He shrugged. "They weren't kissing and it didn't say girlfriend on her shirt, so I don't know."

I watched the front door of Hazel's Front Porch Bakery for the next ten minutes and was finally rewarded by the sight of Grant leaving with a blond woman. I hadn't doubted Darwin, of course, but it was such a strange turn of events that it seemed unbelievable. Even harder to swallow, Grant pointed at the front of my shop and crossed the street with the woman beside him.

"They're coming here," I said to my brother.

"Maybe they need paint," he said.

I cut him a look and then put on a smile as Grant came through my front door. Darwin was right about the blue shirt and the blond hair, but he hadn't mentioned that the woman with Grant was quite beautiful. Knowing him, he hadn't quantified the fact as important.

"Hello, Millie," Grant said. "I wanted to stop in and say hello and also introduce you to one of my colleagues. This is Erin James."

I held out my hand. "Millie Silver," I said. I wanted to ask how she knew Grant and when she had arrived. I was walking on the cool dark sand with Grant just last night. Was Erin waiting for him at the hotel when he returned to it? "And this is my brother Darwin," I said, gesturing at Darwin who glanced up from his smartphone and nodded.

"Erin is my business manager and producer," Grant

said. "I come up with wild ideas, and she somehow finds the money to finance the film."

I smiled. "That must be quite a job," I said.

Erin returned my smile. "It's not that hard to find money if you know where to look, but Grant's films have been getting more and more complicated in the past year or two."

"Wait until you see what I have planned," he said.

"Not the carnival picture, I hope," I said.

Erin turned a questioning glance on Grant and he looked uncomfortable.

"Carnival picture?" Erin asked.

"Millie and I had a moment at the town festival to talk last night and we were joking about the American tradition of creaky carnival rides and questionable food trucks."

We had a moment to talk? He asked me to take a walk on the beach so we could discuss a murder case. How much had he actually told Erin about why he was in Champagne Shores?

"What brings you to town?" I asked.

"Grant, of course," she said. "I'm sure you know he's inherited a large business problem, and he needs someone to help him manage it."

A business problem. It was a heck of a way to say his uncle had been murdered.

Tiffany opened the front door and came in. She smiled at Grant and Erin and paused for a moment right next to them. "Excuse me," she said, sidestepping Erin. "Darwin asked me to help him with a color matching project."

Never in the history of ever had Darwin asked for help matching something.

"My sister Tiffany," I said, pointing to her. "This is Erin James. She's Grant's business manager and producer." They shook hands and Tiffany smiled brightly and then retreated to the back of the store where she picked up a paint card on Darwin's desk and studied it.

I would bet my Aunt Minerva's eight dozen skeins of yarn that she was fake-helping Darwin and he was very confused.

"So, your business problem," I said to Grant. "I'm glad you have someone to help you. Now that the investigation is making progress, you'll want to lay your uncle to rest and get started on addressing his affairs. I'm sure it's very complicated."

"Nothing we can't figure out," Erin said.

Erin seemed like a woman who saw the world in problems and solutions, and I could respect that. I tended to see the world in shades and variations instead, but it didn't mean either one of us was wrong. I was still trying to figure out how Grant saw the world. Since he'd come to Champagne Shores, he'd seemed... confused about how to approach and handle his uncle's sudden demise.

"Is your project on the Gulf Coast all finished now?" I asked Erin. "I believe Grant mentioned he had completed the filming, but do you have lots of loose ends to wrap up?"

"The editing and marketing teams do, but I'm off to the next thing," she said.

"Where will you be filming next?" I asked.

She exchanged a glance with Grant. "That's a good question. Our plans have taken a turn now that Grant's situation has changed. That's what I'm here in town to discuss."

If I had to bet, I'd guess Grant's change in situation was something Erin considered to be a good thing. It was her job to find the money for projects, and now Grant had suddenly found a big golden pot of it. That could mean he needed her help more than ever managing it, or it could mean he didn't need her anymore. It would be interesting to see what happened, even though it was none of my business.

"We're off to start sifting through my uncle's office and his business affairs," Grant said. "Wish us luck."

"Good luck," I said, waving a hand as they went out and got in Grant's red sports car.

Tiffany joined me at the window as we watched them drive away. "I wonder if she'll leave a hair in that car, too," my sister said.

I sucked in a breath. "Really? You think she's a match?" I had been so busy wondering who she was and battling just a smidgen of jealousy that I hadn't thought about her hair being a lot like the one in evidence at the police station.

"I couldn't say for sure, but she's a candidate for a closer look," Tiffany said. "I texted Darwin when I saw her on the street heading for your shop. What a jackpot."

"For the record, I didn't need help matching anything," Darwin said.

I laughed. "I already figured that out."

"Do you know what we need?" Tiffany asked. "We need cookies and wine and girl time."

"Okay," I agreed.

"I'll call Aunt Minerva, we'll grab Hazel and go to the festival for takeout food for dinner. Then we're coming back here and looking through all my new beauty magazines and having fun."

Darwin turned on the paint shaker and we turned to look at him.

"You can come too, if you want," Tiffany said. "At least for dinner."

The paint shaker started clunking louder. "Off-balance," he said. "I'm going to work on this machine and do our weekly computer backup."

"If you're trying to make us jealous, you're definitely winning," Tiffany said.

Darwin shifted his glance to me. "Sarcasm?" he asked.

I nodded. "Afraid so."

NINE

THE COFFEE SHOP, beauty salon, and paint store all closed at five, and I met up with Hazel, Tiffany, and Aunt Minerva in front of my shop. We tried to get together for a girls' night at least once a month, usually coinciding with a movie we all wanted to see, a birthday, or something new in the world of hair, beauty, or fashion.

"I have three bottles of wine in my fridge, plenty of those Italian cookies we love, a stack of new magazines, and a romance movie on my DVR," Tiffany announced. "No one will go home hungry or sad."

"That's a guarantee I'll take you up on," Hazel said. "I'm getting pizza and cheese fries from the food trucks. I swear I can order pizza anytime I want, but somehow it's better from the festival."

"Same with the steak sandwiches," Aunt Minerva said.

"Corn dogs and funnel cakes," Tiffany said.

They looked at me because I hadn't said anything yet. "All of the above," I said. "And I'll still save room for the cookies."

We walked over to the street fair, and I was glad to see the crowd was much larger than Friday night's. It was good for Champagne Shores, even if it was still a town hovering between its orange-stand past and its glitzy hotel future. Saturday was the big day for the festival last year, too, and the most likely to draw tourists from nearby towns in addition to bringing out the locals.

The rides were in full swing, lines were long at the food vendors, and there was plenty of evening left to have fun. Groups of locals, girlfriends and old friends like my group, stood around talking, many of them with a beverage from the beer tent.

The mayor and his wife worked the bottled water station raising money for a local charity, and I saw members of the town council helping at the beer tent and ticket stand. Some owners of other businesses, including several who owned the small hotels, had tents set up where they offered brochures or raffles to promote their business. I wondered how the other hotel owners felt about Herb being arrested. Had their newfound unity against Ransom Heyward survived his death? If suspicion landed on Herb because of his vocal opposition to Ransom Heyward's development, the other hotel owners had to feel they had dodged a bullet and could have just as easily been suspects.

Of course, the other hotel owners had the benefit of *not* having a murder weapon found on their property. I'm sure they were silently breathing sighs of relief just as other residents of Champagne Shores were. Except poor Vera Rivers. If she wasn't involved in the murder, she was a victim of it, too, and I wondered what she would do with a half-renovated old motel.

I saw Mark Prince at the festival with some other men who lived in the Champagne Circle neighborhood. They, too, must be relieved that a suspect in the murder was behind bars because it deflected attention away from their battle with the victim. Mark sat with a group of men at a picnic table, beers in front of them, and a group of women I recognized as their wives sat at a different table.

It wasn't so strange to be separated into groups. I was out on a girls' night, too.

"I have to run over and tell Sylvie I got some new nail polish in yesterday's shipment I think she would like," Tiffany said. "You get in line for food and I'll catch up."

Tiffany walked over to the picnic table where the women who lived in Champagne Circle sat together, talking. There were seven women ranging in age from their twenties to sixties, and I assumed they'd become friends because they lived near each other or maybe because their husbands were friends. An affluent community, I knew that a lot of the women in Champagne Circle didn't work and they had an active social club.

My family was from the middle-class section of town where everybody worked. I caught Tiffany's eye as I looked over and she telegraphed a message to me to get her a steak sandwich and waffle fries by pointing and holding up fingers. We'd been communicating via a tight sisterly bond for years, and she didn't even have to tell me to get cheese on the fries.

I gave her the thumbs up and she went back to talking to Sylvie who sat across from a woman with long blond hair. For a moment, I thought it was Grant's business partner, but there was no way she would have worked her way into a table with locals.

Whatever was up with Grant and Erin, it was a whole helping of none of my business. I pictured him combing through his uncle's office, rummaging through a filing cabinet and trying to guess passwords on his computer programs. Erin, by her own admission, was someone who sniffed out money, and she was likely to find it without straining her eyes when it came to the estate of Ransom Heyward.

"Ready?" Hazel asked. She balanced several foil-wrapped packages and my aunt did the same. I juggled my food and handed my sister hers, and the four of us headed to Tiffany's apartment.

"You repainted," Hazel said when Tiffany unlocked her door and switched on the lights. "I love it."

"Thanks. You'll never guess who helped choose the color," Tiffany said. "It's called cranberry smoothie, but I was only allowed to paint my living room this color."

"The other rooms weren't feeling it," I said.

"Are you tempted to repaint all the time because you own a paint store?" Hazel asked.

"Absolutely," I said. "I have the double whammy of problems. I love color and I love the physical act of rolling out paint onto a wall. I don't even mind taping off the woodwork and cleaning the brushes."

"So how do you resist?" Hazel asked. "I have a terrible time saying no to my own baking, especially when there are leftovers at the end of the day."

I laughed. "I don't always resist," I admitted. "My apartment has gotten smaller in square footage since I moved in because there are so many paint layers on the walls. Sometimes I express my painting love by surprising my friends and relatives with a new room color."

"We never mind," Aunt Minerva said. "Although it usually takes your uncle several days to decide what's different."

"It takes Darwin five seconds and he doesn't usually like it," I said.

Tiffany got four glasses down from an upper cabinet and lined them up on the counter. She uncorked a bottle and poured four even goblets. We each took a glass and sat on comfortable chairs around her coffee table.

"I saw Vera Rivers at the grocery store," Aunt Minerva said. "She was buying tissues and chocolate ice cream."

"Oh," I said. "I feel bad for her."

"Do you think she didn't know?" Hazel asked.

"I think maybe Herb didn't know," I said. "What if he wasn't the one who put that murder weapon in his dumpster? Those things are huge and open. Anyone could have tossed it in there and framed Herb and Vera for murder."

Tiffany's mouth hung open in shock. "Who would do that?" she asked.

"Someone who benefited from the police looking somewhere else," I said.

"I don't know," Aunt Minerva said. "Chief Parker certainly already thought of that possibility, but he still thought there was enough evidence to keep Herb in jail for the weekend."

Hazel opened the package of cookies and poured them out onto a plate.

"I'm still stuck on the blond hair thing," Tiffany said, taking a cookie. "The two best candidates in town don't necessarily make any sense."

"Who?" Hazel asked.

"For one, the woman who was with Grant earlier today. His business manager. She wasn't all that friendly," Tiffany said, "but wow did she have beautiful natural blond hair. No processing that I could see. Impressive, and lucky for her."

"I thought the hair came from Ransom's car," Aunt Minerva said.

"It did," I said. "And it doesn't make sense that Erin would have been with the murder victim the night he died. She wouldn't even have known him because Grant says he hasn't seen or talked to his uncle in ten years."

"Grant could be lying," Hazel said.

"But we don't have a particular reason for doubting him. He's not on trial," Aunt Minerva said.

"Although he does benefit." I felt like a traitor to him even though I hardly knew him.

"Who else benefits?" Tiffany asked. "I mean, really. Are the owners of the budget motels in town really better off because Ransom and his project are both dead in the water?"

"Callous, my dear," Aunt Minerva said, shaking her head.

"Sorry," Tiffany apologized. "But it's sadly true. Would the people who might come and stay in the high-priced King's Ransom vacation homes choose to come to Champagne Shores and stay in the budget motels if the fancy ones weren't there? Probably not, right?"

"Maybe not," Hazel said. "But then what was all the fuss about if the motel owners really had nothing to lose by Ransom bringing in luxury accommodations?"

"They must have believed they were losing somehow," I said. "People believe all kinds of things that aren't true. Like bathrooms can be any shade of yellow," I added, shaking my head. "Always a mistake."

"So our blonde in the car isn't Erin," Tiffany said, going back to the hair topic. "It's Mark Prince's wife."

After she dropped that bombshell, silence fell over our group and we each took an extra long sip of wine.

"You all saw her at the festival, right?" Tiffany asked.

"No one wants to say it," Aunt Minerva said. "But

we're all thinking it. This murder has seemed to me from the start as if there was something personal behind it."

"That's exactly what Grant said the first night he came to town. Of course, he knew his uncle was more than capable of making enemies, so he might have meant that Ransom had personally offended someone."

"What would be more personal than your wife, ahem, spending time with your enemy?" Aunt Minerva asked. "Not much, right?"

"You think Chelsea Prince might have been having an affair with Ransom Heyward?" Hazel asked.

"I don't know," I said. "Mark and Chelsea just went on a trip together last week. Cecil told me that Poppy Russell cat-sitted for them while they were gone. Would a couple on the rocks go on a trip together?"

"Yes," all three of my companions said at the same time.

"Couples therapy," Aunt Minerva said.

"Last ditch effort," Tiffany said.

"Romantic reconnect," Hazel said.

I blew out a breath. "Okay, so Chelsea was driving around with Ransom, Mark found out, killed Ransom, and tossed the murder weapon in a dumpster that wasn't even there until the next day at noon. Sure."

"Now you're making it sound unrealistic," Tiffany said.

"Everything about this is unrealistic. For Pete's sake, a man was clubbed over the head and floated overnight until my dog hauled him in like he was a big stick."

Aunt Minerva pulled a skein of yarn, a crochet hook and a few inches of completed blanket out of her bag. It was a beautiful mint green.

"Who's having a baby?" I asked.

"Cecil's daughter. She's not due for months, but I can't work on that ugly orange and red afghan for too long without getting sour. This is my fun project, and I'm already looking forward to putting a frilly white edge on it."

We all drank to Cecil Brooks and his new grandchild, and then we passed around Tiffany's stock of beauty magazines until we forgot about Ransom Heyward's murder for a little while.

WHEN I GOT downstairs the next morning to do a little work on a Sunday without having to watch the door or wait on customers, I checked my answering machine. There was a message from Grant Heyward asking me to call him about a personal matter. Because I had no actual business with the guy, I didn't see how it could be anything other than personal. He left his cell phone number even though I already had it written down on a business card on my desk.

As I debated whether or not to call him, I wondered about Erin and if she had gone on to the next movie location or was planning to stick around and help Grant sort through the giant muddle. I'd seen his uncle's office, and it was as neat and organized as an office can be. However, his computer files, banking, and any deals he had in the works would be complicated even if they were typed out in clear bold letters.

I had some business sense after running my own store for several years, but no way was I playing in the big leagues like Ransom was. I felt sorry for Grant, inheriting a fortune but also being bequeathed the mess that goes with it.

I dialed his number from the store phone. We weren't quite at the reveal-my-cell-number stage of our relationship, and I decided caller identification could display True Colors Paint Store without committing me to anything. I liked Grant and found him attractive, but the wild circumstances of the week made me want to walk on the safe side of the street.

"I'd like to order one hundred and seventy-five buckets of paint," Grant said instead of saying hello when he answered his cell phone.

I laughed. "What color?"

"Surprise me," he said. "Better yet, make them all different colors."

"Now I'm worried about you. You've been under a lot of stress," I said.

I heard him blow out a breath. "And that's an understatement. Would you be interested in taking pity on me and having Sunday dinner at the home of one of Champagne Shores' first families?"

I knew he almost had to be talking about the mayor, but I wanted to stall for time while I thought about it. "If they were here first, they must be pretty darn old," I said. "You must think my life is really boring."

"You know what I mean." I heard laughter in his voice. "The mayor and his lovely wife have taken pity on a poor urchin whose uncle was murdered one week ago today. They think chicken pot pie and chocolate cake will make me feel better."

"It probably will. Irene is an excellent cook."

"Come with me? Please? Otherwise I'll feel awkward."

I wanted to ask why he couldn't take Erin, but I

didn't want to come off as jealous of his beautiful manager. Which I wasn't, of course.

"Okay," I said, "but you have to be entertaining and tell stories about your adventures in filmmaking or Irene tends to get maudlin about how her twin daughters never come home to visit."

Her daughters were my age, and they had both gone to Orlando to get jobs in tourism. The last I'd heard, they were working in the corporate office of one of the giant theme parks and enjoying life in a much larger city than Champagne Shores.

"I promise to be a one-man comedy show," Grant said. "I'll come over at five thirty if that's okay and we'll go from there."

I agreed, and I thought he was going to hang up, but then he said, "Erin and I attempted to get into my uncle's files on his computer without much success. I heard through the grapevine that your brother is a genius with technology."

"He is," I said cautiously. I didn't want to volunteer Darwin for anything potentially immoral or that would make him uncomfortable.

"I wonder if he might meet me at my uncle's office after dinner tonight. To help me locate, open, and transfer files. I'd like you to come, too."

"Tonight?" I asked. "Maybe this afternoon would be better."

"I really can't," Grant said. "I'm making a quick trip over to the Gulf Coast to check on a few things and grab some more clothing since I think I'll be here longer than I'd planned. I'll barely make it back for dinner even if I hurry."

"I'll ask him," I said. I was glad Darwin would have

time to consider the question, and I knew he probably didn't have plans for a Sunday night. Going after dark one week to the day after Ransom was killed felt a little creepy, but at least I wasn't going alone.

"See you at dinner," he said. "And thank you for trying to help me despite the bad feelings my uncle left in this town. I'm not in a position to ask much, but you've been so nice."

"You can make me a heroic angel figure in your next film."

I heard Grant chuckle as he said goodbye and disconnected. He was capable of being endearing, and he had a movie script writer's timing. Still, I wasn't going to let him go to my head.

That afternoon, I was at the drugstore doing the unglamorous task of getting laundry detergent, toilet paper, and toothpaste when I saw Mark Prince buying a newspaper. He saw me, too, and he could have easily avoided me by turning down a different aisle. I had the impression he wanted to run into me.

"I guess it's good that we're meeting in the daytime," he said, looming over me as I tried to remember if I liked the fresh mint or cool mint toothpaste. It took me months to go through a tube, and I usually forgot. I should associate it with a paint color to help me remember. In the color world, there was definitely a difference between fresh and cool.

"Did you need something, Mark?" I asked pleasantly. For the record, I was very glad we were meeting in daylight in a public place. He was starting to creep me out, even though he hadn't done anything worse than I had. I was snooping at the murder scene on Tuesday night, too, and he could have finished me off then if he'd really wanted to.

"I need everyone in town to stop talking about me," he said.

I tilted my head and tried to look innocent. "What are they saying?" I wanted to ask how things were with his wife, but the last time I'd mentioned her casually, he'd nearly exploded. I made a mental note to try to pry information out of Poppy Russel. Had she happened to notice divorce paperwork next to the cat food in the pantry when she was cat-sitting?

"You know what they're saying," he said. "Herb Rivers is a nice guy, and he couldn't possibly have murdered Heyward even though he hated him."

"What does that have to do with you?"

"People seem to think I'm capable of murder."

"Are you?" I asked.

He narrowed his eyes at me. "I wonder if you're the one spreading the rumors that…"

"That what?"

"Oh, no," he said. "I'm not giving you or anyone else any ammunition. The bungling police chief and his idiot boss the mayor are anxious to pin this on someone, but there are a few things I'd like to tell them about Ransom Heyward that might remind them he was no saint."

Out of sheer orneriness combined with stupidity, I said, "I'm having dinner with the mayor tonight. Is there anything you'd like me to pass along?"

Mark's stony expression turned to flushed-face rage and he spun around, slapped his newspaper on the counter, and stormed out without buying it.

Maybe I went too far, but I was tired of games, innuendo, and everyone acting as if they had something to hide. It would be a relief to spend the second part of the evening with Darwin and computers. If there was anything legitimate hiding in those files, my brother would be likely to find it. And there were never any social games or innuendoes with Darwin.

TEN

"THIS IS A beautiful place," Grant commented as we walked up the curving front sidewalk of the Bell residence. "A lot of Florida homes look either too new or as if they were plunked down on a slab of concrete. This one has character like the ones in the Midwest where I grew up."

"The Victorian homes on this street were built by northerners at a time when the railroad was going strong," I said. "There are only a few like this in Champagne Shores. I think Maurice Bell is from somewhere up north originally, so that's probably what appealed to him about this."

The three-story home had a deep front porch with elaborate spindles that were both a painter's dream and a nightmare. Choosing colors to dress a house as beautiful as this one was the fun part but brushing on all the details took time and patience. It also needed to be done pretty often because the heat and humidity of Florida ate paint for breakfast and wood for lunch.

"They just repainted two years ago, and I got to help choose the colors. I really love the burgundy accents with the cream and green. You should have seen it decorated for Christmas."

I rang the doorbell and Maurice answered in less than ten seconds. "Come in and have a drink," he said. "Irene says dinner needs a few more minutes."

We followed him through the entry way where family photos lined the walls and stood in frames on a table. I didn't pause to look because I knew the people who would be in them. I liked Maurice and Irene's twin daughters, but we'd lost touch in the seven years since we had graduated from high school. Grant took a moment to glance at the pictures as we passed by, but he didn't comment. A staircase with a polished wood banister led upstairs, but we went through to a screened-in back porch off the kitchen. Wicker furniture with deep cushions created a conversation area, and there was already a pitcher of lemonade and glasses on a low table.

This could be the cover of a magazine specializing in gracious southern lifestyles.

"I can get you something stronger than lemonade if you like," the mayor said.

"No, thanks," Grant said. "I'm trying to keep my head clear. Sorting through my uncle's estate, even just on a cursory first glance takes every brain cell I have."

"Anything for you, Millie?" the mayor asked.

I shook my head. "I had a few glasses of wine with my friends last night, so I'll stick to something healthier tonight."

Maurice poured three glasses of lemonade. "How's the sorting through your uncle's papers going?" he asked Grant. "It's none of my business, of course, but if there's anything I can do to help you, just say the word."

Grant picked up his glass and sat back in the deep chair. "It's a mess," he said. "I'm getting an estate lawyer, of course, but I'm trying to go through some of it myself first so I can get an idea where to start. Some decisions have to made right away."

"Your uncle seemed like an organized man to me," the mayor commented.

"He was. Very. But his estate is complicated by the fact that he has six major developments completed and, it appears, passed on to managers. Those managers have a lot of questions about what's going to happen."

"You've talked to them?" I asked. I hadn't thought about how many jobs and lives would be affected by Ransom's passing, but the ripple effect could spread all across the country.

"On the phone," Grant said. "Once they got past the shock, they started worrying about the corporation in general and if the property they manage will be sold."

"What do you plan to do?" Maurice asked. "If you don't mind my asking."

"I don't mind," Grant said, "but my answers are pretty vague. My first goal is to make sure justice is served for my uncle." He put his lemonade on the glass-topped wicker table. "He wasn't a warm and fuzzy guy, and I'm the first to admit I hardly knew him, but no one deserves to be murdered in cold blood."

I thought the mayor looked a little pale when Grant spoke with such force about the crime. It was a shock to all of us, to be sure. And the mayor had been there and seen the body for himself. He'd been kind enough to give me and my dog a ride home in his golf cart, but I would bet he was glad to get away from the murder scene.

"Justice seems to be prevailing," Maurice said. "Herb Rivers is behind bars, and we're just waiting for the results on the murder weapon to come back from the state crime lab. At that point, it's going to be an open and shut case."

"I wonder," Grant said. "I don't know Herb, of course, I don't really know anyone in this town, but it seems strange that he would kill a man over a vacation resort that isn't really competing with his motel. He wasn't targeting the same demographic of vacationers, from what I can see."

"All the hotel and motel owners in town were united," Maurice said. "They saw King's Ransom as a direct intrusion on their business. And don't I know it," he added. "Trying to help your uncle get those permits posted with the local building and zoning office was one heck of a trial for me. Some people in this town, like Herb, fought me tooth and nail."

"It was nice of you to help my uncle," Grant said. "But I still don't see why Herb would kill him, not at this stage of the game anyway. Half-built, King's Ransom seems even worse for the town, especially if we don't finish the construction job."

I thought about the BeachWave Motel and how it was also a construction zone. What would happen to the local landmark? And Herb's wife Vera? Although I loathed the shade of orange disgracing the place, the motel was part of the landscape in Champagne Shores and had been there long before I was born. Was it a hasty act on Herb's part to kill Ransom, and had he taken a moment to think about the fallout and consequences?

"Chicken pot pie is ready," Irene said, appearing in the doorway between the porch and the kitchen. "Come in the dining room, and we'll eat."

We got up and picked up our lemonade glasses and Maurice grabbed the pitcher.

"I'm so glad I settled on a potpie for tonight," Irene

said as she led the way into the formal dining room. The long, polished wood table would seat ten, but half the chairs were removed and placed along the walls. A curved window with a built-in seat graced the one wall, and I remembered sitting there at one of Trina and Trudy's birthday parties when I was a kid.

"Trudy is coming home for a quick visit tonight," Irene continued, "and she loves potpie."

"Will she be here for dinner?" I asked.

"Not until quite a bit later, but I'll reheat some for her."

A tall layer cake sat on the sideboard, and I made a mental note to save room for dessert. I tried not to think about the trip to Ransom's office we planned after dinner. I didn't want it to spoil my appetite.

AFTER A POLITE dinner that swerved from the murder case to the mayor's daughters and back to the vacation development topic, we left the Bell residence.

"I wish we were walking to my uncle's office so I could walk off some of what I ate," Grant said while we were still on the porch. "But it will be dark soon and I don't know my way around town very well as it is."

"I do, but I'm happy to have a ride," I said.

I texted Darwin that we were on the way and asked him to meet us in front of the paint store where Grant's red sports car was parked. It hadn't been as difficult as I had feared to talk Darwin into helping Grant with his computer system. Even though my brother dislikes getting into anyone's personal business or affairs, he likes unlocking mysteries and solving puzzles. I'd sold the idea to him as a challenge, and he'd been in a buying mood.

Darwin folded his long legs into the back seat, interested enough in the project to endure being squeezed into a car, and we took off with Grant driving. He put the top down for the short trip to King's Ransom, and the radio played beach music. Even though I'd grown up in Florida, I never got tired of beaches, beach music, and the feeling of eternal vacation that made the state so popular with tourists.

We drove into the eerily silent vacation development and parked next to his uncle's black sedan, the only other car there.

"I thought Ransom's car had been impounded and searched?" I said.

"It was, but when they finished with it, they brought it back."

Grant pushed the button that moved his car's top back into place and we waited until it clicked and locked.

"Do you know if they found any useful evidence?" I asked. I wondered if Grant knew about the blond hair that was found and if he had any theories about the person his uncle was driving around the night he was killed.

"Do you?" he asked.

We had passed enough questions back and forth, and I decided to share what I knew. It was his uncle, after all. "The only thing I know is that they found a long blond hair on the passenger seat which corroborates the story from Stanley the mosquito sprayer about a woman being with Ransom the night he was killed."

"Who's the blonde?" he asked.

"I wish I knew."

Grant shook his head and took the keys from the ignition. "I can't wrap my head around the thought that his car is mine now," he said, pointing to the black Mercedes. "That all of this is mine."

Darwin had remained silent on the ride to the vacation development. I wondered if he enjoyed the top-down drive with the wind pummeling him in the back seat. It was almost dark, but I knew all Darwin's expressions. He didn't usually like new experiences, but he looked happy. It was probably the thoughts of horsepower and torque that accounted for his half-smile.

"That model has a high resale value," Darwin said, pointing to the black car. "If you don't want to drive it, you could sell it or donate it and write it off on your taxes."

In all my life, I'd heard Darwin offer unsolicited advice about five times. I chalked this one up to the code of men when it came to matters of cars. I'd seen Darwin's car magazines in the mail every month, and I wondered when he was going to invest in something of his own instead of borrowing the hatchback I bought used from my uncle when he retired.

"Maybe I'll drive that one on even days and this one on odd days," Grant said.

Grant led us up the front walk and unlocked the door of the model home. It smelled of air conditioning and construction dust when we walked in. The wood floors shone, but the walls were unpainted and there wasn't a piece of furniture in the place. In its bareness, it was almost a welcome contrast to the heavily furnished and ornate Bell residence we'd just left.

"The office is this way," Grant said. I didn't remind him I already knew where it was because I'd met his uncle there. I also didn't reveal that I'd snooped around looking for personal photos or mementos when I'd been alone for a few minutes in the spare but elegant office. It and a bathroom were the only rooms on the first floor that were painted an eggshell white and furnished, and I hoped there was a comfortable bedroom upstairs that was finished. Ransom couldn't have enjoyed living here otherwise.

He switched on the light and pointed to the computer. "If you can help me find my way around his file management and even get past some password-protected screens, I would really appreciate it," Grant told Darwin.

I wandered to the window overlooking the pond where the water barely glimmered in the last rays of the sun. With the office lights on behind me, the window reflected my brother in Ransom's desk chair. I heard the computer booting up and saw Grant's reflection as he opened drawers and filing cabinets.

"Is there anything I can do?" I asked. I didn't want to feel like dead weight in our search.

"You knew my uncle as well as I did. You could suggest password combinations to Darwin, words you think he might have used. I've tried everything."

"Not necessary," Darwin said.

He wasn't going to explain how, but my brother seemed to know a way around anything on a computer. I was glad he was using his powers for good and not for evil, as far as I knew.

I turned and watched the scene in the office instead of seeing it in reflection where everything looked dark and a little spooky. It had only been seven days since Ransom had died alone in the dark, and here we were trying to pry into all his affairs. Would there be personal information in his computer files somewhere, and would we find out more than we'd bargained for?

"Which files would you like first?" Darwin asked. "I can open files and accounts for you, or I could just rename them and you can come back here anytime and view them. If you have a computer with you in your hotel, I could email attachments or share folders from Ransom's accounts."

"I don't know whether I should be impressed or worried," Grant said. He stood behind Darwin's shoulder and directed him which files he wanted to view. I noticed Grant didn't lean over or get in my brother's personal space, and I appreciated his respect for Darwin. My aunt was the only one who habitually violated Darwin's orbit, and I assumed it was because she hoped that someday he would turn into a hugger.

"The banking file will probably scare me to death, so how about if we change the username and password and I'll log in when I'm back in my hotel room so there are no witnesses to either my maniacal laughter or sobbing, whichever hits me first."

I laughed. "It can't be bad news, can it?"

Grant shrugged and raised his eyebrows. "I honestly have no idea."

"Give me a username and password you want it set to," Darwin said, staying on task.

They repeated this process with Ransom's email, online file storage, and even pictures. Grant pointed, Darwin requested a new username and password, and there was a lot of fast typing.

"I'm surprised the police haven't gone through his records," I said. "Unless they're really sure they know the motive and have the right person behind bars, you'd think they'd wonder if something in those computer files would shed light on why someone wanted Ransom dead."

"They seem to think it's obvious why someone wanted him dead," Grant said. "And for all we know, they've looked through these files already."

"I doubt it," Darwin said. "When the chief has to look at anything digital, he always asks me. I helped with two investigations last year over minor stuff."

"You did?" I asked. "How did I not know that?"

"The chief said I had to keep my mouth shut, so I did," Darwin said.

"I don't think he meant you should keep secrets from your favorite sister."

"I didn't tell Tiffany either," Darwin said.

I laughed even though I didn't know if my brother meant it as a joke. I saw him flash a smile before he returned to his intense focus on Ransom's computer.

Grant sank into a chair next to his uncle's desk. "That's plenty for now. By the time I look through all of that, I'll be looking for directions online to the nearest liquor store."

"If we missed something, we can come back," Darwin offered.

"Thank you. I really appreciate your help, both of you."

Darwin shut down the computer, Grant turned off lights and locked doors behind us, and we got back in his car. The night was dark, and I shuddered, wondering if anyone could be out there watching us. We'd had the lights in the demo house on, and it would have been a beacon to anyone who was watching the place.

"I forgot to ask you if last Sunday's crescent moon

was a waxing or waning moon," I told Darwin, turning around to talk to him in the car as I put my seat belt on.

"Since you don't see any moon tonight, it was clearly waning," he said. "That's why it's so dark now."

"I wondered about it when I was here on Tuesday night," I said.

Grant had started to back out of the space, but he stopped. "You came out here on Tuesday night?"

I took a deep breath. "Yes," I admitted. "I'd heard about the woman in Ransom's car by then and I wanted to see if the muddy footprints near the pond on the other side could be a woman's."

"And what did you find?" he asked, his tone even. I couldn't tell if he was intrigued or irritated that I'd been snooping around and hadn't told him. In my defense, Grant hadn't been in town at the time because he'd apparently been in no hurry to get to Champagne Shores.

I was already in deep, so I decided to go ahead and tell him the rest. "I found someone else out there looking at the murder scene in the dark."

Grant put the car in park and turned in his seat to face me. "Who?"

"Mark Prince."

"Are you kidding me?" Grant asked. "Did you tell the police?"

"I didn't know what to tell them, especially since Mark wasn't any more guilty than I was with what he was doing. If he'd threatened me or tried to kill me then, I would have reported it."

"Then?"

"I ran into him this afternoon at the drugstore and he didn't seem very happy that I'm nosing around."

"Did he threaten you?"

"Not directly."

Grant put the car in gear and rolled forward. "We're all in too deep. I feel like a character in a movie instead of all this being real."

He drove out of the silent empty development. There was just a short stretch of road before we got to downtown. As we passed a side street, headlights suddenly flashed on and a car lurched out at us. Grant made a wild correction and steered off the road into soft sand that grabbed his wheels and spun us. We went up on two tires, and for a sickening second, I thought the sports car was going to roll.

The other car that seemed as if it was going to intentionally T-bone us zoomed away, its engine loud in the quiet still night.

"Everyone okay?" Grant asked, putting his hand on my arm. I nodded, my heart in my throat making it tough to speak.

"Amazing traction control," Darwin said. "I don't think you should trade this one for your uncle's after all."

"What just happened there?" Grant asked. "Is it my imagination, or did someone just try to kill us?"

"I don't know," I said. My heart was still beating wildly and I heard a whooshing sound in my ears.

"That car tried to ram us," Darwin said. "I wish I'd gotten a better look at it. All I saw was headlights out of nowhere and it blinded me."

"Is your car damaged?" I asked.

"The heck with my car," Grant said. "I'll calling the police and we're going to get to the bottom of this before it's too late and someone else dies."

ELEVEN

CHIEF CARL PARKER arrived within five minutes of our call and he parked on the road, lights flashing. We had all gotten out of the car, assured ourselves we were fine, and walked around for a moment or two. My goal was to make sure my legs would still work no matter how shaky they were, and I assumed Grant and Darwin were either doing the same thing or trying to dilute the adrenaline racing through their veins.

The chief's first question was about our well-being, and then he got down to business.

"Can you identify the car?" he asked.

Grant shook his head and looked to me and Darwin. We also shook our heads.

"None of you saw it, but it ran you off the road?" Chief Parker asked.

"It was dark, I was just driving back into town, and lights flashed on and the car accelerated so fast out of the side street I was sure it was going to hit us," Grant said. "I didn't see the color or anything."

"I got a good look at the shape and size of the headlights," Darwin said. "I'm trying to run it through my catalog and come up with a make and model."

"I'm assuming this catalog is in your head," the chief said. I knew he understood Darwin's kind of specialness.

My brother nodded. "I'll keep working on it."

"I'd ask if any of you have any enemies," Chief Parker said, "but that's a tough question right now because this town has turned upside down in the last week. Why don't you come back to the station, and we'll sit down and go through this methodically?"

"Is Herb Rivers still behind bars?" Grant asked.

"I double-checked before I came out here, and the answer is yes. I'll follow you to the station."

Back in the chief's office, Grant, Darwin, and I sat in hard wooden chairs in front of his desk. The chief was not wearing his uniform, and I felt bad that our call had pulled him away from a peaceful Sunday evening at home. I pictured him with his feet up watching television with Sheila and then having to jump up and put his shoes on. He looked as if he'd aged several years in the past week.

"I'm starting with the assumption someone was either trying to kill you or scare you. I'm thinking scare is more likely because it wasn't the most effective way to kill someone. Even if your car had rolled, you would have rolled through sand."

Grant crossed his arms and leaned back in his chair. "I'm not sure that makes me feel any better."

"Keep in mind that last Sunday's murder attempt was a whole lot more effective, I'm sad to say," Chief Parker said. "So this seems more like a warning."

None of us said anything, and I wondered why someone was warning Grant away from being on what was now his own property.

"Which brings me to my next questions," the chief continued. "Which of you was being warned, why, and who was sending you a message?"

Grant glanced at me. "I'm the most likely candidate

because I just walked into my uncle's shoes. But why kill me? No one around here would directly benefit from my death, and I don't think I've made any personal enemies like my uncle apparently did."

"Where did the three of you go tonight?" the chief asked.

"We went to my uncle's office because I needed help getting into his computer files. Nothing illegal, just a matter of my uncle being a little too dead to tell me his passwords. I have to figure out how to start handling his estate, and I also wonder if there is something in those files that will shed light on his murderer."

"I'd like to hear about it if there is," the chief said. "Darwin and Millie were helping you?"

"Yes. Millie and I picked up Darwin after we had dinner at the mayor's house," Grant said.

The chief's expression froze and he looked from Grant to me. "Why did you have dinner with the Bells?"

"He invited me," Grant said. "He said he felt bad Champagne Shores wasn't showing me much hospitality. He's one of the few people around here who seemed to like my uncle, so I thought there wasn't any harm in going. I asked Millie to go along because she's a local and I felt awkward going alone."

"We had chicken pot pie and chocolate cake," I said. I knew it wasn't relevant, but the tension in the room was killing me and I didn't have anything else to contribute.

The chief smiled. "Irene has sent over treats to me and my staff many times. I'm betting dinner was delicious."

"Very," I confirmed.

"Anyone else at the dinner?" he asked.

"No. Irene said Trudy was coming home this evening, but not until later and she planned to heat up left-overs for her. Pot pie is her favorite."

"I'm happy to hear that." The chief sat back in his chair and fiddled with a pen on his desk. The wall clock behind him ticked loudly, and the whole evening suddenly seemed surreal to me. How did Darwin and I end up in the middle of a murder investigation and nearly get killed ourselves? I felt responsible for my younger brother, and sudden guilt over dragging him into this hit me.

"What did you talk about at the dinner?" Chief Parker asked.

I tried to rewind the entire conversation in my head. Nothing really stood out to me or shed light on what happened later in the evening. "We talked about Ransom's murder, of course, and Herb and Vera and how strange it is that Herb would turn out to be a killer. Irene said she was going to send over a casserole to Vera and a key lime pie, which I thought was really nice."

"Anything else?"

"Maurice asked Grant what he was going to do now," I said.

"What did you say?" the chief asked, turning his attention to Grant.

"I told the truth. I don't know where I'm going from here with my uncle's estate," Grant said. "I have no experience with this sort of problem."

"Did you tell Maurice or Irene that you were going out to King's Ransom tonight to go through the computer files?"

Grant glanced at me, head cocked. "I told him I was working on going through them and it was a nightmare, but I don't think we said we were going this evening."

I shook my head. We hadn't talked about it at dinner with the Bells, but the chief's question gave me a creepy feeling. Sheesh. Was everyone in this town suspected of being a criminal? Next it would be my Aunt Minerva. If she had hand-knitted anything for Ransom Heyward, it would have been black. He seemed negative but without passion, and the way we were discussing his death without any emotion made me sad for him.

"What else did you talk about at dinner?" Chief Parker asked.

"Grant told some amusing stories about his films and the places he's been," I said. "We talked about paint colors and how the exterior paint on their house is holding up. I advised Irene not to change the color of the dining room because it's just right, and Irene told us about Trina and Trudy and their work at the theme park. They love it and they're making good money, according to their mom."

"Did you drive or walk to the Bell house?"

"Walked," Grant said. "My car was parked in front of the paint store."

"The whole time you were at dinner at the mayor's?"

"Am I getting a ticket for exceeding the two-hour parking limit?" Grant asked.

"Were you at the mayor's house longer than two hours?"

"No," I said, jumping into the questioning. I flashed a grin at Grant. "Probably only an hour and a half. And those parking limitations only apply Monday through Saturday anyway."

"There would have been plenty of time for anyone in town to notice Grant's red sports car parked in front of your shop," the chief said, looking at me. "If someone wanted to plan something, all they had to do was wait and follow you wherever you were going."

I shivered, imagining someone in town—almost certainly someone I knew—lying in wait for an opportunity to strike a blow at me, Darwin, and Grant.

"I feel like there's a whole other shoe waiting to fall," the chief said, raising an eyebrow at all three of us. "Like there's something you're not telling me or that I'm overlooking."

"Mark Prince," Darwin said. I turned to him, surprised that he was volunteering information. I knew he liked the chief and had helped him with projects, so he must have felt comfortable spilling details and maybe even speculating about the case. "He was rude to my sister this afternoon at the drugstore, he has a blond wife, and he was nosing around the murder scene on Tuesday night when Millie was out there nosing around, too."

"Whoa," Chief Parker said, hands spread on his desk. "That's a lot to dissect."

When my brother decides to open his mouth, he goes all out.

"It wasn't his car, though," Darwin said. "Mark has an SUV, and this was a car, it sat lower."

"What does his wife drive?" Grant asked.

Darwin shrugged a shoulder. We didn't see Chelsea Prince downtown a lot because, even though she had somehow been elected to a seat on the town council, she seemed like the kind of woman who went to a larger city in the region to socialize and shop. Darwin had probably not observed and catalogued what she drove.

"She's got a little blue car, I think. I can run her name and see what's registered to her. First tell me about the snooping at the murder scene," Chief Parker said, turning his attention to me. "And don't leave anything out. You're not the one on trial here even though you may be guilty of some extra curiosity."

"I'm just trying to help," I said. "And I believe you asked me earlier this week to keep my ears open."

The chief smiled and put me at ease. "Guilty as charged."

"It all started with the hair found in Ransom's car. I thought that perhaps he'd had an argument that turned into a crime of passion. I wondered if the scuffle at the murder scene showed any signs of having a female involved. You know, smaller footprints, high heel marks, things like that."

"A conveniently dropped lipstick container with DNA all over it," the chief added.

"Did you find one?" Grant asked, his voice raised with excitement.

"No. Wishful thinking," the chief said. "Do you really think a woman could have bashed Ransom over the head and tossed his body in the pond?"

"If she was provoked," I said. "Anyone is capable of doing things in the heat of the moment."

"Okay," the chief said cautiously as if he either didn't agree or he was starting to wonder about me in addition to everyone else in town.

"So I went to King's Ransom on Tuesday night by myself. I took a flashlight but left Sunshine at home."

"You didn't go?" the chief asked Darwin.

"I didn't know she was going," he said.

"While I was by the pond looking where the yellow tape was, I heard someone else and it was too late to run because I knew he'd seen me, too. So, Mark Prince and I ended up having a conversation at the murder scene."

"And you're just now telling me this."

I swallowed. "I wasn't sure it was relevant, and I got the impression from our talk that he was curious, just as I was."

"Have you talked to him any other times this week?" the chief asked.

I nodded. "We bumped into each other at the bakery, too, and this afternoon at the drugstore."

"Coincidence?" Grant asked.

"It's a small town. It could be. Today was the only day he made me feel really uncomfortable, even though we were in plain view in the toothpaste aisle. He said he didn't like people in town talking about him and insinuated he thought I was spreading gossip."

"Have you?" the chief asked.

"Not really. I only told my family about seeing him at the murder scene. But then when my sister, Aunt Minerva, Hazel and I saw Mark's wife at the festival last night, we went back to Tiffany's and talked it over with the help of a bottle of wine. Tiffany thinks the blond hair is a good match for Chelsea Prince."

"I'm starting to think I have the wrong guy behind bars," Chief Parker said.

"Grant's business manager has the same blond hair that Chelsea does," Darwin said.

Grant's head came up quickly and I saw his look of surprise. "Erin?"

"I'm just saying if we're going by hair color, there are other women who look guilty," Darwin said.

Grant's brow wrinkled and I could see he was trying to make sense of that fact. "Erin had never heard of my uncle until he was killed, as far as I know, so I think we can rule her out."

"DNA could rule out anyone we wanted," the chief said. "But I don't know if we need to go that far right now."

"So what's next?" Grant asked quietly.

"Next, I'll escort you all home. But tomorrow, I'm going to start a conversation with Mark Prince and maybe try another interview with Herb Rivers. He's refused to say much, but I might be able to get him talking if I tell him he may not be the only suspect."

Darwin and I rode in the police car and followed Grant to his hotel parking lot. We waited until he'd safely entered the hotel.

"Do you think you should go in and look in the closet and under the bed?" I asked.

The chief shook his head. "What happened to you on the road was a cowardly scare tactic. I wouldn't expect anything else to happen tonight."

He drove us to our door, reminded us to lock our doors, and Darwin and I went up the staircase to our side by side apartments.

"You'll think of the car," I said. "Just sleep on it."

"The pieces to this puzzle are not fitting into place," he said, shaking his head. "It's going to drive me crazy and it's dangerous."

"Let's see what happens when the chief interviews Mark and Herb tomorrow."

"OH, MY GOODNESS," Aunt Minerva said when she brought lunch to me, Darwin, and Tiffany on Monday. "You will not believe what I heard about the Beach-Wave Motel."

At this point in my life, I would have believed nearly

anything including the motel had once had George Washington and the King of England on its guest list.

"Bedbugs," Aunt Minerva said, dropping the word as if it was a bomb. "Vera has hired a service to come in because they are infested. Absolutely infested."

I took a container of macaroni and cheese, still hot, from my aunt's quilted bag. Tiffany and Darwin did the same, and we all found chairs in the stockroom in the back of my paint store. Darwin couldn't sleep the previous night, so he'd come down and rigged a motion-activated bell on the front door of our shop so we could eat lunch in the stockroom of the store without worrying about missing a customer.

"You could have waited until after we ate to tell us that," Tiffany said.

"Vera told Janet that she and Herb were going to keep it quiet and use it as an excuse to remodel," Aunt Minerva said. "You can imagine what a report of bedbugs can do to a motel's reputation. But now that Herb is in jail and suspected of murder, I guess Vera decided they didn't have anything to lose."

"So," I said. "She's going to eradicate the bugs, complete the renovation, and hope Herb gets exonerated so they can just move into the next half century of motel ownership?"

"I guess," Aunt Minerva said.

"Vera is a remarkably hopeful and resilient woman," I said. "More power to her."

"Maybe it was sabotage," Tiffany said. "One of the other hotels planted the bugs. Maybe it was Ransom, and that's why Herb killed him."

Darwin and I chewed our food and stared at our sister.

"Ridiculous?" Tiffany asked.

"I assumed you were being sarcastic," Darwin said.

"So this is why Herb has kept his mouth shut and refused to say why he's been acting so suspicious," I said. "It hardly makes sense to let yourself be suspected of murder rather than admit you have an infestation."

"Maybe it makes sense if you own a motel," Tiffany said. "Reputation is everything in a small business."

I nodded. "Poor Herb and Vera. That's why they didn't want their dumpster searched. Now I get it. If Herb's not the killer, he wouldn't even have known the murder weapon was in his dumpster."

"Now that the chief knows the killer can't be Herb, maybe he'll get out of jail," Tiffany said.

"Wait a minute," Aunt Minerva said. "How does the chief know Herb can't be the killer? Just because he has bedbugs doesn't mean he's not a murder suspect."

Darwin and I had filled Tiffany in on the events of the previous evening, but our aunt didn't know about the attempt to scare us…possibly to death…and she wasn't going to like it.

"While Herb was behind bars, someone made an attempt on Grant Heyward's life last night," I said. "Tried to run him off the road and roll his car, but he's a better driver than the bad guy thought."

"How do you know about this?" Aunt Minerva asked. "I didn't hear that at the bakery, drugstore, or grocery store this morning. April at the yarn store would surely have told me if she knew."

"We were in the car," Darwin said. "Me and Millie."

"You were what?" our aunt said, her voice rising to trouble-pitch.

"Helping Grant with a computer project," I said, trying to mitigate Aunt Minerva's response. "I went along with Grant to a dinner at the mayor's house, and then we picked up Darwin afterward to go hack into Ransom's computer files. The road incident happened after dark on our way back into town."

"When you say hack into—" my aunt began.

"Nothing illegal," Darwin said. "Grant owns those files now if he's the beneficiary. He just needed help locating data."

"I seriously wonder what Grant might find when he has time to look through those," Tiffany said. "Maybe Ransom had secrets none of us knew about and he was actually killed by the Russian mob."

I admired Tiffany's creativity, and she may have been right about Ransom having secrets.

"Everyone seems to have secrets," I said.

"I narrowed the make and model of the car down to three possible things," Darwin said. "I called the chief this morning and told him, and he was going to run a search through the division of motor vehicles to see if he can find any logical matches."

"I'm surprised you didn't already do that," I said.

"Hacking into the government's computers isn't something I would do," he said.

"Good," Aunt Minerva said.

"Unless I had a good reason or was directed to do so by someone in authority," Darwin added.

We heard the newly installed front doorbell ring. I got up. "I hope it's someone repainting her bedroom who needs help choosing a color. I'd love to think about paint and not murder for the rest of the day."

When I stepped into the store, I discovered it was a paint customer, but not a new one. Herb and Vera Rivers stood at my counter. They didn't look sinister or angry, but I was still glad when Darwin joined me at the counter.

"We're ready to paint," Vera said. "I just bailed Herb out, and he's free for the time being pending further investigation."

"Congratulations," I said.

"Lucky me, the real killer tried to strike again last night," Herb said.

I waited for him to explain, but I suspected he already knew that I knew. The chief had to tell him something, and why not tell the truth?

"And lucky for all of us, he was unsuccessful," I said.

Herb and I exchanged a glance but neither of us continued the train of thought. I'm sure he was just darn glad to be out of jail, even if people in town were still casting suspicion on him. Now that he was released on bail, I knew everyone in Champagne Shores would soon hear what happened with Grant being run off the road. It would probably result in a string of new visitors to my paint store wanting to talk about the hair-raising experience when all I wanted to talk about was satin versus semi-gloss.

"We've decided to do a more complete renovation than we had planned," Vera said. "We're going to take our time with it now that people know about…"

She didn't have to say it, and I wasn't going to make her.

"So, paint?" I asked.

She smiled and nodded enthusiastically, and I guessed she was happy to talk about paint instead of murder, too. "We've had a change of heart about paint colors."

I held my breath, hoping they had experienced a sea change and would consider something other than orange. Or had they gone back to their original plan of keeping the color that had been disgracing their motel for fifty years?

"We're thinking blue," Vera announced. "Several shades. If we're going to be called the BeachWave Motel, we ought to have a color that water comes in."

I waited for Darwin to jump in and explain that water isn't blue. It was the kind of unscientific thinking he usually couldn't tolerate. When he said nothing behind me, I knew he was either engrossed in a computer program, strategic paint shaking algorithm, or had gone back to his lunch.

I smiled at Vera and Herb, thrilled that they had seen the light when it comes to appealing color. In a flash, I reimagined their motel in appealing, hospitable blues that would evoke the seashore and vacation. I hoped it wasn't too late to change their bedspread order so they could eradicate orange entirely from the premises. If the bathroom tile or fixtures were orange, that would be an obstacle, but I'd encountered color foes before and vanquished them.

"Any particular shades of blue?" I asked.

"We're thinking turquoise," Herb announced.

Of all shades of blue. My joy faded like a pillow left in a sunny window, but I maintained my smile and a shred of hope. "Let's go to the color wall," I said, believing I could talk them into something in the neighborhood of turquoise that we could all live with. I began pulling sample cards from the rack and laying them out on the table just inside my sunny front windows. It was time for a new beginning for the BeachWave Motel, but there were too many unanswered questions in Champagne Shores for me to take my usual joy in finding one true color that would work for my customer.

TWELVE

"DINNER?" GRANT ASKED when he called my store late on Monday afternoon.

Maybe it was time to give him my personal cell phone number after all we'd been through in the past few days. If I could be run off the road and interrogated with a guy, I'd like to think it was a precursor to a friendly relationship.

"Not at the mayor's house again," I said.

He laughed. "My hotel has a nice place with an ocean view. Six o'clock?"

"Why not?" I said. "My reputation in town is completely destroyed anyway, and I'm now part of the historic gossip surrounding your uncle's murder."

"You flatter me," he said.

"And it's safer to meet you there so I don't risk riding in a car with you again."

"I'm not sure my ego can handle such enthusiasm from a beautiful lady," he said.

I laughed, assured him I would meet him there, and disconnected.

The last hour of the day dragged on, and I only had one customer looking for varnish to match the woodwork in his living room. Paint is more my passion because color can make a big change, but I respect the beauty of wood and cheerfully help people with stains, too. After I closed the shop, I went upstairs and spent several minutes staring at my closet before knocking on my sister's door.

"I have a dinner date," I said. "Sort of. With Grant."

"Where?" she asked, pulling me into her apartment.

"Hotel restaurant."

"Time?"

"Less than an hour," I said.

"I have just the thing," she said.

I'm in the lucky position of having a sister who is roughly the same size as I am and also has much better taste in clothing. She opened her closet which was organized as if she was planning a visit from a home improvement show. Dresses on one end, blouses on a top rack over skirts and pants neatly draped over hangers. It was even color coded from light to dark and her shoes were displayed on racks as if they were art.

She took out a blue dress and held it toward me. "It's pretty but not date-y," she said. "In case this isn't an official date. You can also wear flats with it so you're covered if you have to run away from murderers or climb out of a trap the killer sets by digging a big hole and luring you into it." She opened the seam on the side. "Pocket for your cell phone, also useful if you're tied to a chair in an abandoned house."

"I'm having dinner at a nice place on the beach," I said. "Not breaking into an abandoned factory where thugs are hiding smuggled weapons in shipping containers."

"You can't be too careful," she said. "Has your week gone as you expected?"

"No," I admitted.

She went to her dresser and selected a bottle of nail polish. "I'll blow out your hair while your nails dry."

An hour later, I arrived at the hotel restaurant in my beautified state, and I was gratified to notice Grant's appreciative glance. Even though our relationship was of the non-dating-murder-investigation-only kind, it was nice to feel attractive. Tiffany had managed to make my long brown hair look mildly glamorous through the magic of heat and brushes, and I had followed her instructions in applying just a bit of makeup.

Grant also looked as if he was ready for a pleasant evening that did not involve murder weapons and unanswered questions. He wore a white collared shirt and dark pants, looking very much like he did the night he first came to town—was it just five days ago?

"Thanks for coming," he said, offering me his arm.

We were seated at a table by the window and the waiter left us with a wine list to peruse.

"I'm thinking of getting an expensive bottle," Grant said. "If you'd like to choose one to share."

"Red or white?"

"Whichever you like," he said. "I started looking at my uncle's bank accounts today, and it appears I can afford anything on that list."

"Was it overwhelming?" I asked. "Trying to make sense of someone else's records?"

I didn't want to imagine what it would be like to try to digest a family member's earnings and spending all at once, especially when you hardly knew the person. If someone suddenly had to view my expenditures and wonder how I spent so much on lifestyle and home décor magazine subscriptions—digital and print—I would feel exposed. I didn't have a lot of indulgent spending habits, but I did find it hard to resist any new hardback books on home design and remodeling. Before and after photos were my secret addiction.

"Painful," Grant said. "Erin is helping me get at least a cursory handle on the situation, but I also left a message for an estate lawyer over the weekend, and he called me back today. I'm going to need help, and he has a team of corporate and finance lawyers who will see me through this, for an outrageous fee of course."

"Worth it," I said sympathetically, nodding.

"The harder part will be his personal stuff. He has a lot of folders, some of which haven't been opened in years and some he opened recently. Judging from the file names, it looks like a lot of plans, ideas, and dreams. He obviously had a lot more projects he planned to build."

"It's a shame," I said. "That he never got to."

Grant looked out at the ocean for a moment. "It's more of a shame that his only legacy is the properties he developed. No family to mourn him at a funeral, not even my parents. I asked my dad if he wanted to have his brother's body brought back to Michigan for a funeral, but he said no."

"There's no one there who'd want to pay their respects?"

"My dad thought there might be some old college acquaintances, but he didn't even know how to contact them and he didn't know if Ransom had kept in touch anyway. My uncle was building a fortune, but I think he was tragically lonely."

"I'm sorry," I said. "It's such a sad situation for you to be in."

He smiled ruefully. "Choose your wine and we'll

drink to him. It's the least we can do, and about the only tribute he's going to get."

Grant and I had a glass of wine before our food arrived, and we talked about things other than the murder of his uncle. I told him about my parents, the little I remembered of them, and how my aunt and uncle had raised me and Tiffany and Darwin after a traffic accident claimed my parents while they were out to dinner on their tenth anniversary. Grant told me about the magical winters in Michigan which he claimed he didn't miss a bit.

"You have your own skis but you haven't used them in years?" I asked.

"And snowshoes," he admitted. "I guess I could sell them online, but you never know when my work might take me to some winter wonderland and I'll wish I had those skis and snowshoes."

"I have a surfboard," I said. "Same idea, right? If I can surf, I can ski?"

Grant laughed. "Probably better than I can, and you don't have to ride a lift or freeze your mittens off. Maybe you could teach me to surf while I'm in town?"

"I can try," I said. "But the ocean is a little cold right now and it tends to discourage beginners. What do you usually do for fun now that you can pretty much choose your locations?" I asked.

"My work is fun," he said. "I love taking a story and turning it into a film. I'd like to think I'm doing some good."

I made a mental note to try to locate one of his films online and watch it. The more time I spent with Grant, the more I found him worthy of research that had nothing to do with his uncle's murder.

"I love home improvement shows," I said. "Maybe we should team up on a project. You can find a building or community center that is hideously ugly, and I can work my magic with paint. The before and after photos and video could put my paint store on the map."

"I can see it now," Grant said, smiling. "The reclaimed gothic mansion that had a revival and now houses orphans and abandoned litters of kittens who will suddenly thrive because the walls are…what color should the walls be?"

"That depends. I'd have to see the place and let it speak to me."

"You have a gift for listening to walls?" he asked.

I nodded. "Just as you have a gift for imagining a story or a cause as a film."

The excellent wine combined with the view of the Atlantic made me feel relaxed and happy chatting with Grant about our pastimes and passions. I hated to go back to my apartment over the paint store after such a nice dinner, and I was considering suggesting a walk on the beach after dinner when an unexpected sight stopped me.

Erin.

She waved at us from the hostess stand, and Grant's expression told me he wasn't expecting her. So much for our walk on the beach. For all I knew, Erin and Grant had shared a dozen romantic evenings and a hundred bottles of wine at sunset.

"What are you doing here?" Grant asked after he'd motioned for her to join us and the waiter had added a third chair to our table for two. His tone wasn't discourteous, but I had the definite impression he was sorry she was interrupting us. Maybe that was just what I hoped.

"Would you believe I came for dessert?" she asked. Grant shook his head. "No."

"I'm sorry about this," Erin said, turning to me with a friendly expression. "It's rude for me to just show up, but I wanted to talk to both of you about some information I found when I started going through the files Grant shared with me."

"Something serious?" he asked.

"I believe so. Serious enough for me to make a three-hour drive to come see you. I'm glad Millie's here, because I think we need the help and perspective of a local person."

I decided the title *local person* was neither an insult nor a compliment. I wasn't sure about Erin, but I still wanted to give her the benefit of the doubt.

"Dessert?" our waiter Jerome asked, standing next to Erin's chair with a tray filled with temptations. "Tonight we have triple chocolate torte, raspberry cheesecake, and crème brûlée for our guests with excellent taste." He smiled and lowered his voice. "We also have key lime pie for the tourists."

I went to high school with Jerome's older brother, so he knew I would be a safe target for his tourist joke. People in Champagne Shores were divided about the future direction of the town and whether it should awaken from its sleepy beachside slumber, but the younger generation like Jerome and people my age knew that tourists brought dollars and provided jobs so we didn't have to move away from our hometown. We could be chasing tourist cash over in Orlando, or we could eke out a living a few streets from where we grew up on idyllic sunrises and lazy afternoons with sand between our toes.

Jerome had to know who Grant was and that he was

far from being just another tourist staying at the twelve-story hotel. Even though I doubted Jerome had seen Erin around, it was obvious that she was there on business, not pleasure. She wore a blue silk sweater, dress pants, and heels as if she'd just come from a meeting. What had she driven to Champagne Shores to tell Grant?

"Triple chocolate torte," I said. "If that tastes as good as it looks, I'm going to regret finishing my dinner."

"Cake for me," Erin said, and Grant added, "make it three."

"Here's what I wanted to ask you about," she said when our waiter had left. "I looked at the permits and land transfers for the King's Ransom estate here in Champagne Shores. It sounds dull, but I thought if I started at the beginning, it might help me put it all into perspective."

"You're either braver than I am or willing to spend more time on this," Grant said. "I didn't even open that file."

She laughed. "You know I'm willing to wade through red tape and jump through hoops. We wouldn't have gotten our last three films made if I weren't."

With her confidence, business experience, and expensive shoes and purse, Erin made me feel like a small-town girl, even though I had excellent hair and nails thanks to my sister.

"Here's the strange thing I found," Erin said. "I know that Ransom acquired part of the property he needed by buying up a street of junky houses and tearing them down. But that wasn't enough. He needed more land, so he also bought what had been a park behind and to the south of the street of houses. It's called Sunset Park."

"I know," I said, glad to have something to offer the

conversation because of my knowledge of Champagne Shores. "I was glad to see those houses go. Even though they were old, they didn't have character. Not everyone felt that way, but people couldn't argue with the price tag. One family refused to sell for a month or so, but then they realized they could get a much nicer home elsewhere in town for the amount Ransom offered."

"And the park?" Erin asked.

"It was hardly a park," I said. "It had a slide, two swings, and a picnic table. I think it was most popular as a graffiti target because the one streetlight near it didn't work."

"It may not have been impressive to you, but Sunset Park was protected property," Erin said. "It had been gifted to the city about a hundred years ago with the stipulation that it could never be sold or developed."

"You're kidding," I said. "I never knew that, and I wonder if anyone else around here did?"

"Someone did," Erin said. "There was a special waver added to the title transfer granting permission for Ransom Heyward to buy and develop the property as long as he included public green space."

"Who issued the waver?" Grant asked. "That's the person who could tell us more about it."

"The city council approved it in a secret executive session," Erin said.

"How do you know?" I asked. "You can't keep your bike combination a secret in this town, not that you need to lock your bike because everyone knows who it belongs to."

"It says so on the title notations. Executive session, change in land use and ownership approved."

"Maybe we need to figure out who's on the town council," Grant said.

"I can tell you that right now," I said. "The mayor, Don Sommers who owns a used car dealership on the north side of town, and Chelsea Prince."

"Mark Prince's wife?" Grant asked. "Are you serious?"

I nodded. "She ran on the platform of beautifying the entrances to the north and south sides of town and prettying up the beach access. She was in the lucky position of having no competition because people in Champagne Shores would much rather complain about problems than have to go to meetings and try to fix them."

"That's not unique to Champagne Shores," Grant said.

"But it's really a serious problem here," I said. "I heard the mayor almost had to bribe two people to run in the election."

Erin picked up our wine bottle and swirled it making it obvious it was empty.

"We can get another," Grant said. "I think we're going to need it."

"Maybe I'll just get a glass. I can't believe this town is so screwed up that people will kill to make their point, but they won't run in an uncontested election," Erin said.

"It sounds bad when you put it like that," I said. "But you're not wrong."

"So the blond hair," Grant said. "The chief called me to tell me there were no matches in the state data base, but that doesn't tell him much except whoever it belongs to isn't a criminal."

"Blond hair?" Erin asked. "Should I be worried?"

Grant shook his head. "There was one found in Ransom's car which may have belonged to a woman who was with him late that night—if you believe Stanley the mosquito sprayer."

"Okay," Erin said, holding up both hands as if there was a beach ball between them and she wanted to keep a firm grip on it. "I think I've got this. Blond Chelsea Prince helped Ransom get permits to build his vacation playland, but then something went sour—possibly while riding in Ransom's car and being discovered by Stanley the sprayer—and she killed him."

"Killed Ransom, not Stanley," Grant said with a small grin.

I blew out a breath and was glad Jerome showed up with three tall pieces of cake on a platter. We each picked up a dessert fork and took a bite. I glanced out at the calm ocean with a hint of peachy purple hanging over it in the last light of the day. So calm and beautiful compared to the maze of facts and accusations we were trying to navigate.

"The husband," Grant said. "He's a much more likely murderer, although it doesn't say much for their marriage that they seemed to be on opposing sides when it came to my uncle. Mark Prince hated the vacation development, and if Chelsea voted in favor of it…whoa, boy, that's a tangled web."

"We should let Chief Parker know about the land transfer and the protected status of the park," I said. "We could also ask Maurice Bell how that waver went through."

"Maurice Bell?" Erin asked.

"The mayor," Grant said. "We had dinner at his house last night and then the evening got really weird."

Grant told Erin about the incident on the road on the way home from the late-night visit to Ransom's office.

"When you emailed and said you had to risk your life to get these files, I had no idea you weren't kidding," she said.

We went up to Grant's suite after dinner and called the police chief. Instead of asking us for details on the phone, he offered to come over and see the documentation for himself on Grant's computer.

I considered leaving instead of hanging around with Grant and Erin, but I felt I should stay just in case I could offer helpful information about the land in question. After all, I had played in Sunset Park as a child. On hot summer days, the slide's shiny metal had burned my backside and I'd dared my sister to fly higher and higher on the side by side swings. I had never appreciated the small park tucked between two alleys, but now I had a wave of nostalgia thinking about the city landmark being bargained over and sold.

"I'm glad you called," Chief Parker said when Grant let him into the suite.

I had never been in any of the hotel rooms at the new SunBeam Resort, but if Grant's room was representative of the accommodations, the other hotels and motels in town had a lot to fear. The window overlooking the ocean was dressed tastefully in an ocean blue curtain. The wall coverings complemented both the scenery and the modern furnishings, and the natural wood floors made it seem more like a beachfront home than a hotel. Perhaps the hotel and motel owners in town had a miserable choice siding with either this new hotel or Ransom Heyward's vacation development. The tension might have driven them to desperate actions.

"We have some interesting information that doesn't reflect all that well on my uncle's morals, but it might help the investigation," Grant said.

"I can't wait to hear this," the chief said, taking the chair Grant offered. I sat on a couch with Erin, and I noticed one of her long blond hairs was loose and clinging to her blue sweater. I desperately wanted to take it and give it to the chief to send in to the state crime lab, just in case. However, I knew it was a ridiculous impulse. She wasn't a suspect. It was Chelsea Prince's hair I really needed to steal.

Grant turned on his computer and gave the chief a quick outline of Erin's research. When the main screen came up, Erin went to the computer and leaned over Grant's shoulder, pointing to the file she'd investigated. The chief, too, got up and looked at the screen.

"Can you send me a PDF of that real estate transfer?" the chief asked. "I'd like to include it with the rest of my evidence. It may be the best thing we've got."

"How about the murder weapon?" I asked. The last I'd heard the crowbar was at the state crime lab.

"It's the weapon all right, even had Ransom's blood on it. But no fingerprints. Whoever tossed it in the dumpster was smart enough to wipe it first," the chief said.

"So we'll just have to get him or her a different way," I said, hoping to sound encouraging.

"I'm trying," the chief said. "Now that Herb Rivers is out of jail and battling bedbugs over at the Beach-Wave, Mayor Bell is all over me to make another arrest."

"Did he have any suggestions?" I asked.

"That would be a peach," Chief Parker said, "but no."

"If the mayor gives you a hard time," Grant said.

"You can always tell him the victim's next of kin is satisfied with the pace of the investigation."

The chief smiled. "I wish that would help."

"I think I'll go home," I said. It was getting late and, given the turn the evening had taken, it was obvious to me that there would be no walk on the beach. At least not for me and Grant.

"I'll take you," the chief said. "And what about you, Erin, did you need a ride somewhere?"

"I'm staying here," she said. "I booked a room before I drove over from Tallahassee."

"Lock your doors," the chief said. "I'll be in touch."

The chief and I were silent in the elevator because there was a family with two kids also going down to the lobby. As we walked outside, I couldn't contain my questions any longer.

"Are you planning to arrest Mark Prince or at least bring him in for questioning?"

"I'd like to, but it keeps looking more and more like his wife ought to be the one answering the questions."

He opened the passenger door of the police car, and I got in. The chief wasn't wearing his uniform tonight, which was probably good because it minimized attention inside the hotel. He drove his police car, though, and I was glad to ride in the front seat just in case someone saw me and reported it to my aunt and uncle. If I were in trouble, I'd be in the back seat.

"Did you find out who owns those models of cars Darwin described?" I asked.

"Three possibilities and a huge database for the state of Florida division of motor vehicles," the chief said. "My contact at the DMV is acting like this is as complicated as programming a spacecraft, but I suspect Darwin could write a program to cross reference the list in about five minutes. I wish I could let him have access to the state's database without breaking the law," he said.

I shrugged. "Maybe it will only take a week, and in that time the killer probably won't strike again or move out of the country."

"Thanks," the chief said. He dropped me off in front of my store, and I grabbed one of my favorite groups of paint samples before going up to my apartment. Talking with Grant about creative projects reignited my desire to do something more than just sell paint and pour out advice.

Even though it was dark, I took a hard look at my kitchen and made an important discovery. It didn't want to be eggplant any longer. I fanned out my samples and chose a much lighter purple the color of lilacs with spring dew on them. When I woke up tomorrow, I vowed to paint a test swatch where the daylight would fall on it. I would follow my own advice and live with the swatch for three days and then my kitchen was going to be spring lilac unless the color disappointed me at any particular time of day.

It would feel like a wonderful new beginning, but I just hoped the murder investigation would wrap up before my three-day waiting period was over so I could savor the process.

THIRTEEN

THE NEXT MORNING, my first customer was Poppy Russell with two cats on leashes. Everyone in town was accustomed to seeing Poppy with cats in tow, but she had never come into my paint store with her furry friends. Unlike some of the rescued cats I'd seen her with, these two looked healthy and confident. Their fur shone in the morning sun and they moved with grace and ease.

I didn't think they were the same cats I'd seen her with a few days earlier, but I'd been so worked up at the time about picking up my lunch from Cecil that I hadn't taken a close look.

"Oops," Poppy said when Sunshine stood in alert stance next to the sales counter and looked to me for instructions. I heard a low whine in her throat and I could see her quivering with excitement, but she didn't chase down the intruders.

"It's okay, Sunshine," I said, putting a hand on her head. "We have company."

My dog looked up at me with her beautiful brown eyes and then she laid down, her ears still perked.

"Saint Sebastian and Saint Fabian," Poppy said as the matching tabbies began exploring. "They're eight years old and they rule the roost at my place."

The two cats stuck together and crouched low to investigate under a cabinet. Poppy bent over to talk to her cats. "Did you see something you like for your new house?"

"Are you moving?" I asked.

"Certainly not. I'm just adding on to the kitty fort that goes from my living room to the screened in porch. These two got to come along to choose the color because they are notoriously opinionated."

Darwin reached down and scooped up a cat. "Which one is this?"

"Saint Fabian," Poppy said.

The cat rested his paws on my brother's shoulder and rubbed his face on Darwin's ear. Despite not being cuddly to other humans, my brother liked dogs and loved cats.

"You should get a cat," Poppy said.

I knew Darwin had been thinking about it, and Poppy's visit seemed fortuitous. "Do you have one looking for a home?" he asked.

"Always. Right now I have a kitten named Saint Anthony who loves to be held. He's black with white feet and a white patch over one eye. He has a very short tail as if he may have been persecuted wherever he came from, but he's very loving."

"Maybe I'll come over and visit him," Darwin said.

"You could deliver paint," I suggested. "Just as soon as Saint Fabian and Saint Sebastian pick something."

Poppy stood in front of the color wall, hands clasped in front of her.

"Can I make a suggestion?" I asked. "I think cats would be happiest with this green." I took a color card and held it in front of Saint Fabian who batted it from his position on Darwin's shoulder. "It's the color of new plants in the spring."

Darwin gave me a raised-eyebrow look because I almost never recommended green for walls.

"They're cats," I said quietly.

Poppy held the card in front of the other cat who had hopped up on the counter. The cat nudged his head against it. "I think that settles it," Poppy said.

I hoped to settle it pretty quickly because Sunshine had gotten up and was flicking her tail and shifting her weight from foot to foot as if she was ready to take off at any moment. Although she was well-trained and accustomed to being hospitable in my shop, it was asking a lot to have two cats nosing around in her space.

"How much paint do you need?" I asked.

"Oh, I have no idea," Poppy said. "The kitty fort isn't like a regular room. It has angles and nooks. Steps, hiding places, even a tower. It's very complicated."

"I could go measure it," Darwin offered. "And visit Saint Anthony."

"What a wonderful idea," Poppy said. "I don't know if I need a pound or a bushel of paint."

I waited for Darwin to explain to her that those weren't standard units of paint, but he was too engrossed in rubbing Saint Fabian's chin.

"Have you been busy cat-sitting for anyone?" I asked.

Poppy shook her head. "Not this week. That's why I have time to do a home improvement project."

"I heard you took care of Mark and Chelsea Prince's cat while they were gone last week."

"Almost two weeks ago now, and they have two cats. Loki and Lexi, both Siamese. I have no idea where they got such strange names, and it took three days for them to warm up to me even though I usually have a gift with cats."

"How long were their owners gone?"

"Only four days, which was such a shame because they got home just as I was making progress."

"I like longer vacations," I said, trying to think of clever ways to be nosy.

"Oh, I don't think it was a vacation," Poppy said. "It was really a long weekend, and they didn't seem happy when they came home. Of course, that could be because," she lowered her voice even though there was only me, Darwin, two cats, and a dog to hear, "I think they're having marital problems."

"Really?" I asked.

She nodded. "It looked to me like someone had been sleeping in the spare bedroom, and it's just the two of them in that house. When I asked if they'd had house-guests, Chelsea snapped at me like a cornered kitty."

"Goodness," I said. "I hope they didn't have bedbugs like the BeachWave Motel."

"I wouldn't think so," Poppy said. "That house was immaculate inside, and one of my tasks was to run the sweeper every day to pick up any stray cat fur. I shouldn't say anything, but I noticed a brochure for a couples retreat on the kitchen counter, one of those fixer-upper retreats."

I tried to keep a neutral expression, but my brain was like the inner workings of an old-fashioned clock with all its gears turning. Mark and Chelsea and their potential marriage problems could easily fit with the theory that it was Chelsea with Ransom Heyward that night. It also explained why Mark had snapped at me a week earlier when I'd mentioned his wife.

"When would be a good time for Darwin to come and measure the kitty fort?" I asked.

"I'd like to get started on my project as soon as I can," Poppy said.

"I could come right now," Darwin volunteered.

I nodded and made a mental note to prepare for Saint Anthony, our new shop cat. When Darwin left a moment later with Poppy, each of them with a cat on a leash, I knelt down and rubbed Sunshine's ears.

"You were the best girl," I said. "And I think you're about to get a new playmate."

An hour later, Darwin had still not returned, and I imagined him wedged into the cat fort with a tape measure playing with twelve cats. Cherry Steele came in and bought paint for her porch floor. I already had it mixed and ready for her because she'd called ahead just as she did every spring. Bob Younger who lived three houses down from my aunt and uncle came in with a piece of fabric. His wife wanted to repaint their bedroom and she loved the color of the little blue flowers in the fabric. He was on his way to the hardware store for curtain rods, and I asked him to stop on his way back and I'd have a sample ready for him.

Chief Parker was my next guest, but he wasn't looking for paint.

"Darwin around?" he asked, coming in and taking a seat at my paint counter.

"He's been kidnapped by Poppy Russell and a herd of cats."

"Poor sucker," the chief said. "Want me to send help?"

I shook my head. "He's probably loving it. What can I help you with?"

"It's about the headlights," he said. "The three possible cars didn't cross-reference with anything interesting in this county, so I broadened the search and started plugging in last names of anyone in Champagne Shores I could think of."

"Did the computer come up with Chelsea Prince?" I asked. My head was all wrapped around her couples retreat with her husband who was sleeping in the spare bedroom.

"No, she doesn't have a car on the list Darwin gave me."

"Oh," I said, disappointed.

"But you'll never guess who does," the chief said.

"Don't tell me Herb and Vera Rivers have one of those cars parked behind their motel."

"Trudy Bell," he said.

"The mayor's daughter?"

He nodded. "The mayor's *blond* daughter."

My mouth fell open. "Trudy was coming home that evening we had dinner with the mayor." Chief Parker and I stared at each other and I could hardly readjust my train of thought to accommodate this shocker. "I can't believe this. I went to high school with her and Trina. How could she run me off the road and nearly kill me?"

"Wait," the chief said, holding up both hands. "You can't jump to conclusions based on hair color, proximity, and the shape of her car's headlights."

"Sure I can," I said. "What are we going to do next? Have you talked to the mayor? Poor Irene, she'll be devastated if it turns out that her daughter is a murderer."

Chief Parker leaned an elbow on my counter and slumped. "To say that I have to proceed carefully is the world's biggest understatement. I haven't talked to the mayor about this, and I can't think of a clever way to get a hair sample from Trudy to compare with the one

I sent to the lab. And even if I did, proving she was in Ransom's car that night doesn't prove she killed him or tried to kill you."

"I wouldn't want to be you right now," I said.

"I don't want to be me, either."

The front door opened, the motion-activated bell rang, and Darwin came in with a black and white kitten tucked under his arm. Sunshine jumped up and ran to him and he snuggled the kitten close while rubbing the dog's head.

"Saint Anthony," Darwin said, holding up the kitten for us to see. "But I'm calling him Tony."

The chief grinned. "Poppy Russell strikes again."

I held out my hands for the kitten and took him. He was irresistible, and I didn't blame my brother for bringing him home. "We can find you a sunny pillow by the front window," I told our new pet. I put my hands over Tony's ears. "The chief has some news, but I don't want your new kitten to hear it and become jaded about humanity."

"Did you find the owner of the car?" Darwin asked.

"I think so, but it's going to be touchy," the chief said.

"Why?" Darwin asked as I kept my hands over the kitten's ears.

"The mayor's daughter Trudy has that model of car registered in her name in Orange County where she lives now, but she was home on Sunday night."

"Wait a minute," Darwin said, rubbing his eyes as if he was going through his brain catalog. "She has blond hair."

"I know," the chief said. "What I don't know is how I'm going to haul her in for questioning without losing my job and my mind."

Aunt Minerva showed up with a big quilted casserole container at five o'clock. It was bowling night for Uncle Foster, so our aunt came alone with what smelled like the family favorite cheesy ham and potatoes.

"I just talked to Gladys," she said. "She said Mark and Chelsea Prince were in the police station today and they talked to the chief for an hour. When they left, Gladys asked Chief Parker if they were suspects, and he said they had rock solid alibis for each other."

"I wonder why he questioned them now that we think it's someone else," I said.

"What are you talking about," Aunt Minerva asked. "Who do we think it is?"

I sighed. "Come upstairs with the casserole. I'll lock the door, and then I'll tell you and Tiffany all about it. Darwin already knows."

As I walked toward the front door, I heard my aunt say, "Who is this?"

Tony the kitten had taken up residence in Darwin's desk chair. Unwilling to disturb the kitten, Darwin hadn't sat down in hours.

"Poppy Russell gave him to me," Darwin said. "I named him Tony."

I heard my aunt cooing over the kitten while I locked the front door and then we all trooped upstairs for a family dinner. We ate in my kitchen and everyone weighed in on the small patch of lilac paint I'd run upstairs and swiped on during a lull in the middle of the morning. I told Aunt Minerva and Tiffany all about the chief's visit and the car being a potential match for Trudy Bell's.

"But Trudy is the nice one," Tiffany said. "Trina was always the snobby twin. I'll bet this is one of those cases where one twin commits a crime and blames the other one and because their DNA matches, the good twin goes to jail for life."

We all looked at Tiffany, even Tony who yawned and curled into Darwin's side.

Our aunt related her entire conversation with Gladys who worked front desk and dispatch at the police station.

"What do you think their rock-solid alibi is?" Aunt Minerva asked. "Can married couples be alibis for each other?"

"I think so," I said.

"Then I wonder why Vera Rivers didn't vouch for Herb's whereabouts the night of the murder," Tiffany said.

"I think they were both being sketchy on the details because of the bedbugs," I said.

Tony woke up and scratched his ear vigorously.

"He doesn't have bedbugs," Darwin said when we all looked at the newest member of the family. "He's very clean."

"This doesn't make any sense," Aunt Minerva said. "Trudy Bell doesn't even live in town anymore, and why on earth would she kill Ransom Heyward? I still think it's Mark and Chelsea Prince."

"Maybe," I said. "But without evidence…"

"We could get some evidence," Aunt Minerva said, "and then maybe Chief Parker would have to listen."

"What are you suggesting?" Tiffany asked.

"That it'll be dark in an hour, your uncle won't be home until late, and I could use a walk through a nice neighborhood like Champagne Circle to walk off the carbs in the casserole we just ate."

"We could walk anywhere," Darwin said. "The beach would offer more resistance if you really wanted to burn calories."

"Oh, Darwin. Just put your kitten to bed, put on a dark shirt, and meet us back here in a few minutes," Tiffany said.

"That's my girl," Aunt Minerva said.

"I don't like this," I said. "I already went snooping once, and it scared the stuffing out of me."

"You have experience," my aunt said. "We need you."

I sighed and went to my closet for a dark sweatshirt. "Bring me one, too," my aunt called from the kitchen, and I grabbed her a lightweight navy-blue pullover. Casserole night was taking an unappetizing turn.

My phone rang, and I didn't recognize the number. "Should I answer it?" I asked Tiffany and Aunt Minerva. They both shrugged as we stared at the ringing phone.

"Hello?" I said cautiously.

"Millie," a cheerful voice said. "Matt Riley from the newspaper. I heard there have been some developments, but I'm not getting much from the police station and my editor is looking for an updated story on the murderer now that it seems the cops are closing in."

"I'm sorry, Matt," I said, rolling my eyes at my aunt and sister. "I don't have any information or comments for the newspaper. Your guess is as good as mine."

"That's disappointing, but I hope you'll call me if and when something goes down. You have my number."

"I do, but how did you get mine?"

"I'm a reporter. We can find out just about anything."

"Well then, I wish you would find out who killed

Ransom Heyward so Champagne Shores can get back to vacation."

Matt laughed and said goodbye, but his phone call left me feeling uncomfortable. Were we really getting closer to an answer, and how dangerous would it get before we found one?

Less than an hour later, it was fully dark when Tiffany, Darwin, Aunt Minerva, and I set off from the back entrance of our building. I left Sunshine home alone again because I was afraid she might bark and give away the clandestine snooping the Silver family was about to do. Sure we could claim we were out for a pleasant walk on a balmy evening, but I doubted any of us could pull off an innocent expression if we were pressed.

"I hope Tony won't be lonely," Darwin said. "It's his first night in a new home."

"We'll be home by dawn at the latest," Tiffany said.

I didn't even have to see Darwin's face to know what he was thinking.

"She's kidding," I said. "We'll be back in less than an hour."

We took the backstreets to the Champagne Circle neighborhood. Without a bike or car, it was a solid ten-minute walk at a brisk pace. My aunt had frequent cardio classes on her side and the rest of us had youth and adrenaline. Two-by-two, we took to the sidewalk in the upscale neighborhood and our steps synchronized. We moved quickly and quietly until we paused one house away from the Prince residence. Darwin had looked up the address before we left home just to be double sure, and the number on the mailbox confirmed it when Tiffany swiped the beam of her flashlight across it.

"Now what do we do?" Aunt Minerva asked.

"This was your idea," I whispered.

"I thought we might see them through the window, maybe arguing about the murder or her affair with Ransom."

We all looked at the house where lights were clearly on but quality window treatments prevented us from seeing in.

"The cars," Tiffany said. "Darwin, are you sure those headlights don't look like the ones that ran you off the road?"

Two cars were backed into a garage, but the big garage door was open.

"Give me your flashlight," he said.

I noticed that the flashlight was really a small promotional penlight with the name of my paint store on it. I handed them out as free gifts to customers.

Darwin shaded the beam with one hand while creeping closer and examining the car's headlights.

"Well?" Tiffany asked.

"I don't think so," he said.

"Give me the light," Tiffany said. Aunt Minerva and I shrank into the shrubbery edging the driveway while Tiffany used the beam to peer in the driver's window.

"What are you doing?" I whispered.

"Hoping for a hair stuck to a headrest," Tiffany said. "I think I see one. I'm just going to—"

A squealing sound shattered the night and all of us jumped. It took a moment for me to realize it was a cat.

The door from the house leading to the garage opened and Chelsea Prince leaned out.

"Lexi?" she called. "Come inside."

She flipped on a flood light covering the garage and

driveway area, and all four of us ran like crazy. I hoped she hadn't gotten a good look at Tiffany next to her car or the rest of us on the edge of the driveway. Aunt Minerva took the lead and raced back the direction we'd come, all of us running flat out. We didn't stop to catch a breath until we were clear of the Champagne Circle neighborhood and in the dark quiet streets behind Ransom's incomplete project.

"I think my shoe's untied," Aunt Minerva said, "shine your flashlight on it so I can tie it."

Tiffany was silent.

"Oh, no," I said. "Did you leave it there?"

"I must have dropped it when that cat scared the crap out of me, and who the heck is Lexi?" Tiffany asked.

"The cat," I said. "Poppy told me. Their cats are both Siamese named Lexi and Loki."

"I wonder if they saw us?" Darwin asked.

We heard a police siren wailing.

"I'm guessing yes," I said. "Back to my place, fast and silent."

The four of us race-walked the side streets back to the rear entrance of my building and dashed inside. I closed and locked the door and we trudged up the stairs, breathing heavily.

"Drink," my aunt said.

"We need to rehydrate after all that running," Darwin said.

"Not that kind of drink." Aunt Minerva went straight to my fridge when I opened my apartment door and got a bottle of cold wine. Darwin went next door and fetched his kitten, and we sat in my living room looking as if we'd gotten called to the principal's office. Sunshine licked Tony's ears and sat next to him, waiting for the kitten to do something interesting.

"Maybe they didn't see us, and maybe they won't find the flashlight I dropped," Tiffany said. "And we weren't guilty of anything worse than a little light trespassing."

We heard knocking on the street door below. Heavy, insistent knocking. We all froze except my aunt who picked up the wine bottle and drank directly from it, finishing it off.

My home phone rang and I saw Chief Parker's name in the caller window. I took a deep breath and clicked to answer.

"Good evening, Chief," I said in a voice that sounded like a bad actress in a high school play.

"You're home," he said. "That's a point in your favor."

"Make it ten points," I said. "I'm feeling lucky."

"Are you alone?"

"Nope. It's casserole night, so my aunt is here along with Tiffany and Darwin."

"Mind if I come up?"

"There's no more casserole and my aunt just polished off the wine," I said.

"No disrespect to Minerva's cooking, but that's not why I'm here," the chief said.

"I'll be right down."

I disconnected, and Darwin got up. "I'll let him in." Sunshine followed him out the door and we heard her padding down the steps behind Darwin.

Tiffany, Minerva, and I waited, afraid to say anything or even look at each other. In just seconds, the chief was standing in my living room. He scanned all our faces, and then picked up the kitten from the sofa cushion.

"Mind if I sit down?" he asked.

I nodded, and the chief sat down and put the kitten in his lap. "There was an attempted break-in at the Prince home about a half hour ago."

"Goodness," Aunt Minerva said.

The chief flicked a smile at her. "My two officers are over there pretending they know how to fingerprint the car and write a report, but I made an excuse and left with the only piece of solid evidence from the scene."

He pulled the penlight with my paint store's name emblazoned on it from his shirt pocket.

"Of course, there are plenty of these floating around town. It's good advertising, and I think there's even one of these in the everything drawer in my kitchen."

"They're pretty handy," I said, finally finding my voice when I realized the chief almost certainly knew we were the culprits but he didn't seem to be in the arresting mood.

The chief sat back and stroked the kitten's fur. "What were you looking for?" he asked.

"Officially," Tiffany said, "we were out for exercise because dinner was so good we all over-indulged."

"Understandable. And unofficially, you seem to think I must be missing something and if you go snoop around the easiest suspect we've got, you might come up with something to help me out."

None of us said anything, and Sunshine put her nose on her paws and groaned.

"You don't have to say it. I'm not going to lie, when I

had Mark and Chelsea in the station earlier, I was darn disappointed by their answers and their alibi. There's a lot they're not telling me, but nothing amounts to a case against them that would stick."

"Did you ask Chelsea about the executive session at the council meeting when Ransom got the deal on the park?"

"Yes, but she claimed executive session notes are sealed for a reason and I'd have to have a warrant to get that information."

"Very helpful," I said. "Are you going to get a warrant?"

"Probably. I keep thinking there's something I'm missing, and I want to be careful which trees I shake," the chief said. "And whose garages I enter illegally."

"Okay," Tiffany said. "I was looking in the car window to see if one of Chelsea's hairs was stuck to the headrest so you could send it in to the crime lab. Can you believe she's one of the few women in this town who has never been in my salon, so there's not a prayer's chance I have one of her hairs stuck under a chair or curled up in a corner."

"Don't you clean?" Darwin asked.

"Every day," she said, "but hairs get everywhere. Wait until Tony starts shedding and you find cat hair in your refrigerator and stuck to socks in your drawer that you don't even wear."

Darwin looked horrified and I almost laughed for the first time in the past hour.

"Truth be told," the chief said, "I wish you had found something, even though it wouldn't be admissible in court. I'm at a dead end where the only choice is a road I don't want to take. I can't tell the mayor I'm arresting his daughter on suspicion of murder and menacing just because she's blond and owns a car that may or may not be the same make and model as one used in a potential crime. There has to be more."

FOURTEEN

IF IT WEREN'T for the antics of Tony chasing a string and Sunshine trying to play with the kitten, the mood in my paint store would have been thunderstorm gray on Wednesday morning. Ransom Heyward had been dead for a week and a half, and there seemed to be no progress on solving the case. My efforts hadn't panned out and, if anything, had almost made things worse by risking getting arrested along with the rest of my family.

My uncle didn't know what he was missing while he was blissfully bowling at the alley on the north side of Champagne Shores, and I wondered how much Aunt Minerva told him when he got home that night.

"I'm getting treats," I told Darwin. "Do you want the usual?"

"Of course I do," he said.

I should have known.

"Good," Hazel said when I entered her bakery. "I need your opinion about how to repaint."

I stood up straighter. Painting was my superpower, no matter how powerless trying to meddle in the investigation had made me feel.

"I would have come over to your store, but I was too busy this morning. I have good news," she said. There were a half dozen customers in the shop. They drank coffee and had plates of pastries in front of them. The glass-fronted case usually filled with treats was nearly empty, and I had a moment of panic when I realized my favorites may be sold out. I could adjust, but it would be tough on Darwin.

"Is the good news that a group of people who love baked goods has cleaned you out?" I asked.

"Second day in a row," Hazel said. "It's the big hotel on the beach, the SunBeam. Their pastry chef was sick yesterday, so they sent someone here to stock up for the morning continental breakfast they put out for their guests in the lobby. I think my fresh, homemade goods may have outshone their own pastry chef, because they came back again today to shop and also placed an order for tomorrow. Their manager is coming to talk to me this afternoon about negotiating a standing order for the hotel."

"That's fantastic," I said. "A baker's dream come true."

"I know, but it puts a hitch in my plan to repaint because I don't have a lot of time. With the new hotel business, I can't close my bakery while I'm painting," Hazel said.

"I see the problem," I said. "The ceiling is going to be the tricky part. You'll have to set up scaffolding, and even if you hire a painter, it'll be several days at least just for the ceiling."

"Don't be mad," Hazel said as she picked up a waxed paper and began choosing items for me from the bakery case without having to ask what I wanted. In a moment of selfish delight, I saw two cinnamon rolls still in the case. "But I'm thinking of skipping the ceiling," she continued. "I'm just going to leave it off-white and hope it doesn't clash with the creamy white I'm putting on the walls."

"Oh," I said. "It's your store, and I can understand why you need to get this project done and reopen right away." I tried not to sound disappointed that she was abandoning the porch feeling evoked by a blue ceiling. "Time is money, right?"

"Right," Hazel said. "But I have a compromise. Since I already bought the light blue paint for the ceiling, I'm going to use it on the tables and chairs instead of the ceiling."

I glanced around. Mismatched wood tables with a variety of wood chairs gave the bakery a haphazard but eclectically fun vibe. However, all at once, I pictured the tables and chairs painted the same color…and I liked it.

"That may be even better," I said. "I like painted furniture, and you can do a few every evening without having to close at all."

"Think you might come over and help me?" she asked.

I smiled. "Only if I get to eat all the leftover baked goods."

Hazel poured two coffees and put cinnamon rolls in a bag for me and Darwin. She put a dog treat in a separate bag.

"All the leftovers you want," she said. "I've never painted furniture before."

"The secret is sanding and preparation. You want to get off any old varnish so it doesn't interact with the latex paint."

"You're the expert," she said.

"I'm repainting, too," I said. "My kitchen is getting a new color as soon as tomorrow."

"But I liked the dark purple," Hazel said.

"I liked it, too, but I like Lilac Dew for spring and summer."

I thought about the hope I'd had that the murder would be solved by the time the three-day waiting period for my paint swatch was over, but it was looking more and more hopeless.

"You have a visitor," Hazel said, pointing across the street. Grant Heyward was standing in front of my glass window tapping with his finger on the glass. "What's he doing?"

"I believe he's playing with Darwin's new kitten," I said.

"All the more reason to like him," Hazel commented. "I mean in addition to the zillions of dollars he just inherited."

"I think those dollars came with a price, so maybe I'll take an extra roll and coffee for the poor guy."

Hazel laughed and added to my order, and I went back to my shop where Grant held open the door for me. "I met your new friend," he said, pointing to Tony.

"He's Darwin's, but he seems to like everyone."

Grant said hello to Darwin and we all got a roll from the bag. I took a bite, but then dug Sunshine's treat out from the other bag and gave it to her. Tony was staring out the front window, so we didn't have to feel bad eating in front of him. Since he was new, he didn't yet know that magic food came from across the street. Sunshine had figured that out a long time ago.

"I didn't get in touch with you yesterday because I was in the middle of a project," Grant said.

"Film project?"

"No," he said, shaking his head. "Safe-cracking project at my uncle's office. Did you know there are professional safe-crackers who will either use brains or brawn to get into a safe for you?"

"Which did they use?"

"Brains," Grant said. "And they charged me a pretty penny."

"I could have taken a shot at it," Darwin said.

"I wish I had thought to ask you. Which brings me to why I'm here now." He pulled two flash drives from his pocket. "There were documents, cash, a passport and assorted other things you would expect in the safe, but also these two flash drives."

"What's on them?" I asked.

"I don't know. They seem to be encrypted or locked, and I can't even see what files are on them."

"It must be something good," I said, licking maple icing off my fingers.

Grant laughed. "I don't know what's good or bad these days. It could have a big picture of a murderer with a caption that says, 'if I'm found dead, here's your man' or it could be his tax records going back a decade."

"That would still be interesting," I said. "The tax returns would tell you a lot about his business practices."

"Do you want me to open the files on the flash drives?" Darwin asked. "It may take some time, but I can probably do it."

"Thank you," Grant said. "That's exactly why I came to see you."

I tried to reject the tiny feeling of disappointment that he hadn't come to see me. If there was a minor flirtation between me and Grant, it kept getting caught up in and overshadowed by his uncle's murder. *Obviously.* I wanted to whack myself in the head with a paint roller when I thought about being slightly jealous of justice being a priority.

"I have to drive over to the Gulf Coast and meet with Erin and a man who's financing our next film, so I'll be gone all day. If you find anything interesting, call me." Grant looked at me and smiled his movie-star smile. "You have my number."

After he left, Darwin held the flash drives in the palm of his hand, but he had a confused expression on his face. "If Grant just inherited a lot of money, I wonder why he needs to meet with someone who will finance his next film. Can't he finance it?"

"I don't know," I said. "Films are expensive, and maybe his uncle's money will be tied up for a while in court."

I didn't say it aloud, but I also thought it was possible he was meeting with Erin for another reason, and he didn't want to say it in front of me. Was there something between them? Either way, it reminded me how little I knew about him. Was I naïve for trusting him and blind to something right in front of me? He could be entangled in a romance with Erin, and they could have plotted together to kill off his uncle and use his money to build their documentary film empire.

"Do you know what's still bothering me about Ransom's murder?" Darwin asked.

"The fact that it's unsolved?" I asked.

"Of course. I hate riddles without an answer or puzzles with a missing piece."

This was true. I vividly remembered one Christmas when we were younger. Darwin had gotten a jigsaw puzzle with pictures of the planets on it. He put it all together in record time on the dining room table, but when he got to the end there was a missing piece. We launched an epic search of the entire downstairs of the house, but we were forced to conclude that it was a manufacturer's defect. Darwin wrote a strongly worded letter on his Star Wars stationery, and the company sent him a new puzzle, but I think the experience may have scarred him for life.

"What's really bothering me is that no one benefited from it," Darwin said. "People kill because they get something, but who gets something out of Ransom's death?"

"People also kill because they're angry," I said. "And Ransom didn't have many friends in town."

"How did killing him solve a problem for someone else?" Darwin asked.

I sat on the edge of the desk and Sunshine put her head on my knee. Nothing made sense, and I would have loved to have walked away from the entire thing, but I was in the middle of it. "I don't know. Maybe there's an answer on those flash drives. Before you start to work on them, will you mix me a gallon of semi-gloss Lilac Dew? My three days is up, and I'm painting my kitchen this evening."

"Without the benefit of daylight?"

"It's not the riskiest thing I've done lately."

Darwin mixed a gallon of paint and printed a label for the lid as he always did. After that, he worked on and off for several hours on the flash drives. When I asked him how it was going, I got long convoluted answers about downloading a program, writing some sequence, and running a script to unlock and rebuild the tables on the drives. It was a mystery to me, and it reminded me that I was very lucky someone with his genius seemed content for now to mix paint and help me run my store. I hated the thought of him ever leaving, but I knew someone would try to lure him away with a giant paycheck one of these days.

"Whatever is on there seems to be pretty important to Ransom if he went to all this trouble to keep it hidden," Darwin said. "I almost wonder if I should stop now before I see something I shouldn't."

"Grant wouldn't have given it to you if he didn't trust you," I said. "He knew you were likely to see what's on them, and that's his point of having the files opened. He said to call him if you found anything interesting, so he knows you're going to look. Just do your best."

Tiffany brought us lunch because she was on her way back to town from a shopping trip at a beauty supply store. She usually closed on Wednesday mornings so she could go shopping, restock her store, or even have time to do her own nails. Over our chicken sandwiches and fries, I told her about the flash drives Darwin was trying to unlock, and I could see her imagination taking flight before she even opened her mouth.

"I bet it solves the whole mystery," she said. "There could be incriminating photographs, a treasure map, or even clues like in a scavenger hunt. There might even be a video of Chelsea Prince threatening to tell her husband about their affair if Ransom doesn't buy her a diamond tennis bracelet. I can picture her being a tennis bracelet kind of gal."

"Ransom was being held for ransom or bribed in some way?" Darwin asked.

"Not a funny pun," I said.

"I wasn't kidding," Darwin said. "Someone could have been blackmailing him, and that someone could have killed him. Although that's self-defeating because you cut off your cash supply then."

"Unless the person you were blackmailing was about to expose your secret past which revealed you to be a member of a high-profile crime family," Tiffany said.

I sighed and turned to Tiffany. "Before we all turn into either detectives or serial killers, I'm going back to my gravitational center and painting my kitchen tonight."

"Paint therapy," she said.

"Healthier than drinking and cheaper than shopping."

"You're not wrong," Tiffany said. My sister laughed. "I have to go open up my shop for my first appointment after lunch. I'm dreading it a little because Della always wants a hair color that is not right for her and she won't take my suggestions."

"I can sympathize," I said. So many times, people had walked out of my shop with a gallon of paint that I knew would be a mistake before it even hit the wall. My aunt had advised me and my sister that we had to let people make their own mistakes, but it was a tough pill to swallow.

All afternoon, I wandered restlessly around my shop. Darwin worked on the flash drives while also continuing his usual cycle of shaking paint cans and moving them around on the shelves. I amused myself for a while by selecting a paint card for each person involved in Ransom's murder. I chose colors based on my opinion of that person, wrote their name on the card, and arranged them on a desk in the back where no one would see them.

Red for Ransom, the victim. Orange for Herb Rivers.

My aunt would disagree about orange because she considered it a negative color. We liked Herb, but after years of owning an orange motel, I just couldn't assign him any other color. Passion pink for Chelsea Prince and a startling hurt-your-eyes blue for her husband Mark. I included Chief Parker with a strong and soothing navy blue, and I chose a cool gray for Maurice Bell. I selected gold for his daughter Trudy because it matched her hair and I couldn't figure out how she fit in to the story otherwise.

Grant was my last pick, and I went with paper white. He was a blank slate to me, an unknown before the murder and an unknown for the future. I arranged and re-arranged the paint samples, trying to establish a connection between all the players. What if there was someone else involved, a whole palette of colors I hadn't even considered?

When closing time finally came, I had never been so relieved to turn off the lights and lock the front door. Color always soothed me and provided perspective, but there was nothing even the most beautiful shades could offer when there was clearly a missing piece.

"Are you going to stay here all night working on those flash drives?" I asked.

"I'm running the script now," he said. "It's at forty-two per cent, and it will take a while."

"I'll be upstairs painting," I said, picking up the can my brother had mixed for me. "Let me know if the name and address of the murderer is filed under M."

Upstairs in my kitchen, I set up a step ladder, pried open my paint can, and poured a generous amount into a paint tray. I had a new roller and edger, but I planned to use my trusty old paint brush that had been with me for years thanks to careful cleaning and care. I could get a new one anytime, but I considered the brush to be an old friend.

Sunshine curled up on her dog bed by the couch, I put on some music, turned on all the lights, and edged a section of wall. Right before I rolled on the first satisfying swath with the roller, Darwin came into my apartment with his laptop.

"It's a bunch of pictures," he said. "Files and files with pictures of vacation homes, construction sites, and even hotels."

"No file named *secret baby* or *my nefarious enemies* or *why I'm a target*?" I asked. All I wanted to do was transform my kitchen into Lilac Dew because it was far more productive than beating my head against the wall of Ransom's murder investigation. Even his own nephew was off visiting on the other side of the state, so why was I so concerned about it?

"Most of the file names are a place and date, most of them in the past fifteen years," Darwin said as he sat at my island with his laptop. "There are a few random files dated almost thirty years ago."

"Thirty years ago Ransom would have been in college or just out," I said. "Those wouldn't have vacation developments on them."

"I'm still working on the other drive. My computer downstairs is running that through the script right now."

"I'm holding my breath," I said. I rolled paint on my wall and felt the glorious satisfaction of transformation. Eggplant purple, which I had loved for more than a year, was giving way to the spring. A new beginning. I could use a fresh start after the last week and a half of general chaos.

"That's weird," Darwin said. "I tried opening the old one from thirty years ago, but it's password protected. Why on earth would it be password protected in an encrypted file and locked in a safe?"

"Those must have been some fabulous college antics," I said.

"I'm going to check on the other computer," he said.

Darwin left and I tried to ignore the open laptop on my kitchen island. Whatever Ransom was hiding in those files, it may have been the thing that got him killed. But it was hard to imagine something thirty years ago could have any relevance now.

I much preferred to enjoy the glow my kitchen was getting from the fresh lilac paint instead of fussing over a crime that made no sense.

"You won't believe this," Darwin said, holding up a sheet of paper as he came through my apartment door. "The other flash drive had a password folder on it that had passwords for this drive. I guess someone was betting it was unlikely that someone could unlock both flash drives."

"They didn't see you coming," I said.

Darwin sat down and went through passwords for about two minutes until he finally gave a grunt of satisfaction. At least one mystery was unlocked so he might be able to sleep tonight.

"Where did he go to college?" Darwin asked. "There's snow and big old buildings in most of these pictures. I can see a guy in a lot of them who looks a lot like Ransom."

"Michigan," I said, getting down from my ladder so I could look at a picture or two. "It's where Grant is from and his parents still live there." Darwin was right about seeing a younger version of Ransom, but why would he carefully encrypt photos from his carefree college days? I went back to my painting, not being all that sympathetic to college antics. I'd kept my nose clean and my head buried in my classes because I wanted to finish my degree quickly and dive into my dream of having my own paint store. Tiffany had done an accelerated cosmetology degree, and Darwin had done most of his course work online while living at home. The frat boy lifestyle was like a glimpse into an alien world for us.

"These guys behaved like morons in college," Darwin said. "They're throwing snowballs, burying each other in snowdrifts, skiing with beers in their hands—I don't even know how they do that—and there's a picture of them pushing a car out of a ditch. At least I think that's what they're doing. It's dark and the picture is lousy quality." He leaned closer to the screen. "It looks like there's someone in the car but maybe she's asleep."

He put his chin in his hands. "I don't think we're going to find the smoking gun in these folders."

"I didn't have much hope, but thanks for doing all that work anyway."

"I'm going to go check on Tony. I made a little bed for him, and I want to see if he's found it and likes it. Be right back."

Darwin left, but the laptop screen was facing me and the pictures were on scroll mode. I picked up my paint can to refill my tray, and my eyes fell on a picture that was only on the screen for a moment but there was something familiar about it. It was two men in graduation caps and gowns standing in front of a tall stone college-hall-type building. One of the men resembled

Grant, but then I realized it must have been either his father or Ransom because the picture was older.

The other man in the picture caught my attention, but then the picture disappeared and was replaced by the next photo of a large group of young men, perhaps a fraternity or athletic team. I had paint on my hands and was afraid to touch Darwin's laptop, so I went back to my work. I loaded up my roller with lilac paint and started on the wall with the window in it. Why did that other man look so familiar to me?

Darwin came back when I was halfway through the wall, and I asked him to rewind through the pictures. He hit the back arrow over and over while I stood behind him. I started to think I had imagined the picture, but it finally appeared.

"That one," I said.

Darwin stopped the scroll and the picture remained on the screen.

"I'm sure that must be Ransom Heyward," I said, indicating the man on the right in the picture.

Darwin nodded. "He's in most of these."

"And does that other man look familiar to you?"

My brother studied it, and I searched my memory. Where had I seen a picture a lot like this one with that same distinctive ornate building in the background?

Suddenly, it hit me. At the mayor's house, the foyer table with framed photographs. There was a graduation picture of, presumably, the mayor and his parents. I had glanced at it in passing many times without paying much attention, but I was almost positive that the man in this picture was the same.

"It's Maurice Bell," Darwin said. He had come to the same conclusion I had, so I was sure my hunch was correct. I would bet my brother had facial recognition software installed in his brain along with a map of every place he'd ever been and a chronological list of his birthday presents back to age two.

"Bingo. We're looking at a picture of Ransom Heyward and Maurice Bell from thirty years ago," I said. "But it seems really weird, doesn't it?"

"They must have gone to college together, but were they old friends? I never heard anyone talk about them knowing each other in the past, and even though it seems like I'm not listening, I hear every word that's said in the paint store," Darwin said.

I smiled. "I suspected that."

"I don't know what this means," Darwin said. "If anything."

"It means that there's something we don't know. For example, if they were old friends or even acquaintances, why didn't either one of them say so? I had dinner at Maurice Bell's house on Sunday night and we talked about Ransom's murder and never did he say, oh, by the way, we were fraternity brothers back in the day."

"We don't know they were fraternity brothers," Darwin said.

"I was extrapolating," I said. "But it's clear they were at least good friends because you don't have your graduation picture taken with someone you hardly know."

"We should call Grant," my brother said. "Before we look at any more pictures or dive deeper into any of these protected files that are now an open book."

"You're right," I said. "He needs to see these pictures for himself, and maybe he can find out what relationship there was between his uncle and Mayor Bell. Maybe he knows and he hasn't told us for some reason."

"Why wouldn't he tell us something important like that?" Darwin asked.

"I don't know."

I called Grant, but I got his voicemail. I left a message asking him to stop by and see me and Darwin as soon as he got back into town. Darwin closed his laptop and went back to his apartment, and I continued painting until my kitchen was lilac and my muscles and brain were too tired to worry about old pictures and recent murders.

As I closed my eyes that night, I chased away thoughts about the case by imagining instead how fresh and beautiful my kitchen walls were going to be the next morning when I woke up and the sun slanted through my apartment's windows.

FIFTEEN

GRANT CALLED MY cell phone at just past seven the next morning. I was already out of bed, showered, and examining my paint job from the night before. The color was magnificent, a breath of spring glowing in the morning light through my windows. My apartment faced east, and my building was just tall enough for me to see the ocean over the buildings across the street. It was an idyllic place to live in a town that had also been peaceful and friendly until ten days ago.

"I would have called last night, but it was late when I got back," he said. "I turn my cell phone off when I'm driving so I'm not tempted to violate the law and expose my own lack of talent for texting and driving."

I had wondered why he hadn't called, but I had also needed time to process the information about his uncle and mayor while painting my kitchen.

"You might want to come over and see what Darwin found on those flash drives," I said. "I could tell you over the phone, but I want your impression to be pure instead of me telling you what I see."

I knew I could be wrong about seeing Maurice Bell in those pictures, although I had a hard time believing Darwin could be wrong, too. Still, we needed a fresh third opinion before we went in a direction likely to be filled with dark twists and turns.

"That sounds intriguing," Grant said. "I just went

for a nice run on the beach, so I'll get a quick shower and be there soon."

He clearly hurried over because when Grant arrived, I had just unlocked the front door and turned the closed sign to open.

"I'm dying to see what you're talking about," he said.

Darwin had his laptop and his desktop computer booted up and he was ready to show and tell. He began with a lengthy explanation of the procedure he used to unlock and read the data on the drives, and then he explained that he'd found a document with passwords. A person would have to have both flash drives to unlock the mystery, and Darwin cleared his throat and announced that he had. I was very impressed that Grant had remained silent and patient through the explanation because I wanted to just get to the new evidence, and I'm sure he did, too.

"Photographs," Darwin said, "lots of them. I scanned through many of the files trying to get a sense of how the file names matched the data. Most of it isn't very interesting unless you like looking at pictures of floor plans, houses, and developments that all pretty much look the same."

"I may take a look at those eventually," Grant said, "to help me better understand Uncle Ransom's vision so I can figure out how to carry on in his place."

"You plan to try to run his business?" I asked. The last time I had asked Grant about his future plans, he didn't know. *What had changed?*

He shrugged. "I feel like someone has to, it was the only thing that defined his life, and it would seem wrong to let it end with his death."

"In addition to the house and building folders, there

was also an older folder, much older, from about thirty years ago," Darwin said. "It didn't seem to fit, so I opened it and we looked through some of the pictures last night."

"Sorry," I said. "We didn't like invading your privacy and getting in your business, so we only looked at some of them and turned it off and waited for you."

Grant laughed. "You didn't have to be so sensitive to my feelings. Those aren't my pictures or my secrets. I don't think there are going to be any baby pictures of me or revealing photos that will offend me."

"I think there might be some revealing ones, but you can be the judge of that," I said.

Darwin opened the college files and plucked his kitten out of the chair so Grant could sit down. "Just use the arrow key to move through them," he instructed.

My brother and I stood behind him as Grant clicked through the pictures. "Just college stuff," he said. "Ransom as a much younger man having fun. It looks as if he had friends back then. It must have been before he got so bitter and threw himself into his business." He scrolled silently for a few minutes looking at the same ones we'd seen with snowball fights, group pictures, and casual photos taken in what looked like a dormitory lounge. There were beer bottles in most of the pictures, and it looked to me like there had been some wild times in his youth.

"What did you see that caught your attention?" he asked. "Or should I just keep going until I find it?"

"A little farther," I said.

Grant clicked through a few more pictures, including the one in which the boys were pushing a car out of a snowy ditch. Finally, he got to the graduation pictures.

"Here's my uncle with my dad on graduation day," Grant said. "My dad is a few years older and was probably already working by then."

"Did he go to the same college?" Darwin asked.

"No. They didn't seem to travel in the same orbit then or now." He moved to the next picture. "Here's dad and Ransom with my grandparents. They looked a lot younger then," he said, smiling. "They're both gone now, which is maybe just as well. They weren't close to Ransom, but his murder would have devastated them anyway."

I swallowed, thinking about how sad it was that there was no one to be devastated by Ransom's murder.

"Ransom and his friends at graduation," Grant said, scrolling fast. "More friends, more friends with beer bottles in their hands, and…" He paused, staring at a picture of Ransom and another man. "I feel like I know this guy," he said. "But I don't know any of my uncle's friends. There's something…"

"That's the picture I wanted you to see." I leaned in and took another look for myself in the clear light of morning. What I had seen last night was still right in front of me. "We both recognized the other man."

"So it's someone in Champagne Shores?" Grant asked. He leaned in and looked. "Wait a minute. You don't think this is the mayor, do you? Maurice Bell? He's older now, but I could swear…"

"I think you'd be right," Darwin said. "I did some digging on the mayor last night and found some older pictures of him online. There was a twenty-fifth anniversary announcement of him and his wife in the paper a few years ago, and it included their wedding picture."

Grant handed over an article with a wedding picture he had printed. "It's the same guy."

Grant sat back in the chair and the kitten jumped onto his lap. "I'm processing," he said. "Ransom knew Maurice in college, but in all my conversations with the mayor, he never mentioned that. Even though he had opportunity. So, why not?"

I shook my head. "I don't know. Maybe they had a falling out over the years and weren't friends anymore?"

"Then why was Bell helping my uncle? It seems as if someone certainly was helping with those permits and the plans to annex an outer street in Champagne Circle I found in his papers."

"There were actual plans?" I asked. "Rumors have circulated, but it seemed so far-fetched and impossible."

"Nothing's impossible when you have the town government on your side," Grant said. "But this still makes no sense. Why was Maurice Bell so anxious to be helpful to Ransom?"

"Ransom was paying him off?" I suggested.

"There would be records somewhere of those payments," Grant said. "I haven't looked at all his finances, and heaven knows it's so complicated I could be missing it, but it still doesn't sit right. I've said all along that this case seems personal."

We were all silent for a moment. Sunshine snored softly, and the kitten jumped down and went over to the golden Labrador lying in the morning rays coming through the front window. Tony curled up with Sunshine who opened one eye and closed it again, demonstrating her extreme tolerance.

"I did notice something unusual in the saved files,"

Darwin said. "One of them had been opened recently and resized."

"Resized?" Grant asked. "Why would someone do that?"

"A common reason is because it makes it easier to email," Darwin said.

Grant spun around in his chair and looked at my brother. "Which picture?"

"I'll show you," Darwin said. He leaned over the computer and did a quick search by date. "This was resized last Saturday. The day before Ransom died." He opened the file and it was the picture of the car in the ditch.

"What's so special about this picture?" Grant asked. "It looks like this car slid off the snowy road and there are several boys pushing it back on. There's a woman in the front seat, but it looks like she's sleeping through it."

"Who are the men in the picture?" I asked.

Darwin zoomed in on the faces of the two men. They wore hats and coats, and the darkness made the picture quality fuzzy, but I recognized them both anyway. Ransom Heyward and Maurice Bell.

Tiffany came in the back door. "I saw Grant's car out front and thought maybe someone had the grace and foresight to provide coffee and doughnuts," she said. She stopped and looked at the three of us with our grim, puzzled faces. "What's going on?"

"Look at this picture and tell me what you see," Grant said.

Tiffany looked and then recoiled. "I see a dead girl in a car."

"What?" Grant looked more closely. "Do you really think she's dead?"

"Her eyes are closed, and it looks to me like the nap of eternity. I do hair for the funeral home in town here, and you don't want to know the details, but I've seen my share of corpses."

"I...uh...have some thoughts," Grant said. "But I need a question answered first. If this picture was recently resized and possibly emailed, I'd like to know who emailed it to whom."

"We could check the sent items folder in your uncle's email," Darwin suggested.

"Millie," Grant said, turning to me. "Can you spare Darwin for an hour so he can come to my uncle's office with me? I didn't get into his email folder yet, and it's all still stored on that computer."

"Sure," I said. "Of course."

"I have a suggestion," Tiffany said. "You go along, too, Millie. I'll watch your store for you."

"What about your beauty shop?"

"I'll put up a sign that says I'm right next door in case of a hair emergency."

Darwin grabbed his laptop and both flash drives, and we got in Grant's red sports car.

"Déjà vu," Grant said.

"I hope not," I said. "We're in the daylight now."

In just minutes, we were at Ransom's office in the model home. The construction site was silent and abandoned. The only movement was the yellow caution tape near the pond that had come loose and was flapping in the breeze.

"I feel dirty even digging into these old secrets," Grant said. "I'm starting to form a hypothesis that isn't pretty."

"Maybe we should call the chief and ask him to meet

us here," I said. "He might be very interested in this, and maybe he knows something helpful."

"I doubt it," Grant said. "If he'd known anything about my uncle and the mayor, he would have either said something or acted on it himself."

Grant sat at his uncle's desk and booted up the computer.

"I bet there's a desktop icon for his email, and it's not even password protected," Darwin said. "People are more careful about locking down their phones than their email. Fools."

I made a mental note to check the security of my personal email, even though I wasn't going to admit it to Darwin.

"I'll be darned," Grant said. "I'm in."

Darwin shook his head. "Pathetic."

"I'm checking the sent mail folder," he said. "This is sadly easy. There's an email right on top which means it was the last one. It was sent last Sunday to Maurice Bell." Grant looked up at me. "It has an attachment."

Darwin and I stood behind Grant as he clicked on the email. There was no subject line, but the body of the message said *Remember that night? I do.* Grant double-clicked the attachment and brought up the picture of the ditched car on the snowy road.

"I think it's time to call Chief Parker," I said.

Grant nodded and pushed away from the desk.

"The pieces are starting to fall into place for me, but we still need some phone calls and research," I said. "Would you mind going back to my paint store and we'll ask the chief to meet us there?"

"I'll need my computer," Darwin said, nodding.

"In case I need to…research something that isn't… readily available."

Grant blew out a breath. "Fine by me. I just want someone to connect all these dots before my head explodes."

"I think we're getting close," I said.

I called Chief Parker on the way back to my paint store and asked him to meet us there. He didn't hesitate and didn't ask questions.

"Be there in five minutes," he said.

I called Aunt Minerva and asked her to come run the paint store so we could hunker down in the back and work through the details of the murder case. She arrived within fifteen minutes with my uncle in tow, and they assured me they had it covered unless someone needed paint mixed. I told them to yell if they needed me, and then joined Grant, Darwin, Chief Parker, and Tiffany in the back room of the True Colors Paint Store.

Darwin moved his computer to a folding table in the stock room and ran an extension cord and cable for the internet. He grabbed the cordless phone, and we were set up. I closed the door, and we all looked at each other for a moment. Surrounded by boxes of painting supplies and cans of paint, we were going to solve the case once and for all.

"My paint samples," I said. "Be right back."

I went out to my desk and grabbed the paint sample cards on which I'd written the names of all the involved parties. There was a bulletin board in the stock room, and I cleared it off.

"Let's go," I said.

Grant and Darwin took turns explaining the flash drives to Chief Parker and what they'd found in addition to the wedding picture of the mayor and the sent email from the day Ransom died. Working together, we moved my color samples around on the bulletin board to paint a picture of what might have happened. I had to run out front for more samples to represent King's Ransom, Champagne Circle, the park, and finally the scene of the murder: the pond. I chose a tranquil green for the pond because I wanted to think Ransom would rest in peace despite the dangerous game he'd been playing.

Tiffany's imagination and Darwin's computer skill came in handy, but I ran the evidence board and kept the conversation moving.

Aunt Minerva brought in lunch and dropped it off just after noon while Chief Parker was on the phone with the police in the college town where Ransom and Maurice had gone to school. He smiled and nodded at my aunt. We continued working and talking out our theories and evidence until late afternoon when Chief Parker finally sat down and put his elbows on his knees.

"I think we're ready," he said. "I need one more favor out of you, Millie." He handed me the phone. "Invite the suspects to meet us at the murder scene at five o'clock. If you tell them you know who did it and you want their help to prove it, they'll come. No one could resist that."

"Even Trudy Bell?" I asked.

He shook his head. "We'll leave Maurice's family out of it as long as we can."

SIXTEEN

THE CHIEF WAS absolutely right. At five o'clock, I stood
on the bank of the pond where I had found Ransom
floating just over ten days earlier. I had made only three
phone calls, but there were fifteen people gathered at the
scene of the crime with me. Aunt Minerva and Uncle
Foster, Darwin, Tiffany, Grant Heyward, Erin James,
Mark Prince, Chelsea Prince, Herb Rivers, Vera Rivers, Maurice Bell, Chief Parker, and his two police officers. At the last minute, the chief had decided to invite
the reporter Matt Riley who had been with me when
we discovered the body and would be there when we
named the murderer.

Everyone had arrived a few minutes before five,
most of them in cars, but Mark and Chelsea Prince had
walked and the mayor had driven up on his golf cart.

"I'll get right to it," Chief Parker said. "With the help
of Millie Silver and her family, I'm ready to name a suspect in the murder of Ransom Heyward."

"It's about time," the mayor said.

I admired his bravado, but I noticed no one else said
anything. The mood was tense as we stood there in the
late afternoon stillness. I had no idea how the chief was
going to play this, but I knew it wasn't his first time revealing a murderer's identity.

Matt Riley snapped a few pictures and then got out
his voice recorder.

"From the beginning, I have treated this as a crime of either opportunity or passion," the chief said. "Opportunity always comes into play when you're dealing with a victim known to be wealthy or powerful. Ransom Heyward was both. He brought money to this town, and he also brought potential even though not everyone saw it that way."

"That's true," the mayor said, nodding. "He could have put us on the map."

Chief Parker didn't appear to hear the mayor, and he looked to me to continue.

"So," I said, "at first we looked at who would benefit from Ransom's death and the potential end of his project. There were plenty of suspects, people who'd spoken out against the project, people who felt threatened by it." I looked at Herb and Vera Rivers as I spoke. "Even people who represented nearby neighborhoods and didn't like the encroachment, present and future," I continued, now looking at Mark Prince.

"You've got nothing on me," Mark said.

"Hold that thought," the chief said. "When it comes to opportunity as a motive, you can't do much better for a suspect than the person set to inherit everything," he said, looking at Grant. I was impressed that Grant kept a completely neutral expression. Even though I knew he wasn't guilty, I would have squirmed under the chief's gaze.

"Aside from opportunity, the other motive was passion," the chief continued. "Hate or love. That's a messy road to go down. In the hate category, we had Herb Rivers, Mark Prince, and about a dozen other people in Champagne Shores. The love category was a whole lot smaller. Millie got along all right with Ransom, the mayor tried helping him out, and then there was Chelsea Prince who could use her position on the town council to vote in Ransom's favor."

"That's enough," Mark said, stepping forward, his hands fisted. "You stay out of my personal business."

"So it was her hair found in Ransom's car," the mayor said. "We all heard there was a woman with Ransom that night. Stanley never was too good at keeping his mouth shut. So, it was your wife? That's quite an interesting situation, isn't it, Prince?"

The thing about inviting rats to a feast is that they'll destroy each other to get to the good stuff. I wanted to shrink back into the crowd, and I pitied Chelsea and Mark Prince.

"I wasn't at those two council meetings when you voted through the zoning changes and approved the plans for King's Ransom," Chelsea said.

"You weren't?" Mark asked. "But you said you were outvoted by the mayor and Don Sommers."

Chelsea looked at her feet and shook her head.

"Where were you those nights?" Mark asked his wife.

The mayor laughed. "Out with Ransom Heyward, I'd guess."

Grant glanced at me and his expression was grim, almost sick. We had suspected Ransom had used Chelsea to get what he wanted, but he'd been even more devious than we thought. It was sad and wrong.

"There was a blond hair found in Ransom's car. But Chelsea wasn't the only blonde I suspected," Chief Parker said. "I also briefly considered your daughter Trudy." He looked at the mayor and his perfectly timed shot hit its target. Maurice's nasty smile at the problems with the Prince marriage faded and he reddened. "But I'll get to that later," the chief continued.

"You wait just a minute," Maurice said, shaking a finger at the chief.

I wouldn't necessarily have taken the shot across the mayor's bow, but it was effective in removing the painful spotlight from Chelsea and Mark Prince.

"Evidence, scant as it was, started to steer me," the chief said. "The murder weapon was found in the dumpster at the BeachWave, and Herb and Vera refused to say much in their own defense. It almost seemed too easy, but I didn't have anything else at the time."

Herb coughed and I saw Vera squeeze his hand.

"They've got bedbugs," the mayor said. "A motel full of them."

I doubted this was news to anyone, and public sympathy had turned in the direction of the beleaguered motel as soon as Herb got out of jail. Maurice Bell just ended up looking like a jerk with his statement.

"So," the chief said. "We knew Ransom was bludgeoned with a crowbar, probably from a construction truck, and shoved in the pond. We knew that murder weapon was deposited the next day in the dumpster. We knew there was a report of a woman with Ransom the night he died, and a blond hair was found in his car. That hair had no DNA matches in the state database which tells us its owner has no previous record. There were no fingerprints on the murder weapon which tell us the murderer took some time to cover his tracks."

A gull flew low over us and landed on the pond. I looked at the faces around the circle and saw an absolute gamut of emotions. Matt Riley held up his voice recorder, taking in the entire proceeding.

"When Grant finally got into his uncle's computer files, his associate Erin—"

"Also blond," the mayor cut in.

"We noticed," I said. "Erin found some interesting information. Part of the land Ransom acquired for his development was protected by an old deed. It was supposed to remain a park and could not be sold by the city. It *was* sold, and for a song. Chief Parker had a judge unseal the records from the executive sessions where our town council approved that sale and another meeting where they approved the future annexation of more land. There were two out of three council members present, and the motion passed."

Chelsea and Mark exchanged a grim look, and I was afraid their cats were going to be dividing their time between two different households after this meeting was over. The mayor shifted his stance and rocked from foot to foot.

"I still had questions about that action," Chief Parker said. "Mayor Bell is widely known for thinking of the future of Champagne Shores and getting local residents to go along with change for the better. He's been part of the campaign to beautify downtown, improve the city parking lots by the beach, and advertise this vacation town in local and regional magazines. He's done a lot for Champagne Shores."

"Thank you," the mayor grumbled. "You know it wasn't easy."

Chief Parker turned and faced Maurice Bell. "I know you made sacrifices. Big ones."

My heart was thundering in my chest. I knew what was coming. The two junior police officers in town had chosen to stand next to the mayor, and at least half of the people at the pond probably didn't think it was strange. They were on his staff, after all, since the mayor was technically in charge of law enforcement and all city operations.

I took a deep breath and steadied my voice. "Last Sunday night after a friendly dinner at the Bell residence, Darwin, Grant and I were nearly run off the road on our way back to town from a visit to Ransom's office. We had been looking into his computer files, and a car came out of nowhere. Darwin identified the make and model of the car by the shape of its headlights, and the chief ran it through the state database. The only local resident who owns such a car is Trudy Bell."

"My daughter is innocent," the mayor said. "How dare you!"

"I know she's innocent," Chief Parker said. "*You* were driving her car. She came home for a visit later that evening, and her car was probably behind yours in the driveway. You couldn't take your golf cart if you wanted to intimidate another driver, so you made up a reason to leave home and you took Trudy's car."

"I don't know what kind of a game you think you're playing," Maurice said.

"And you had every reason to want Grant and me and Darwin to drop our investigation," I said. "You were probably afraid we would find some carefully encrypted files belonging to Ransom. When you heard us talking about going to Ransom's office as we left your porch, you saw your opportunity."

"Your meddling has gone far enough," the mayor said. "We all know Prince did it. He was getting revenge for Ransom dating his wife. You shouldn't have let Poppy take care of your cats," he said, turning to

Mark. "She told anyone who asked that someone in your house had been sleeping in the spare bedroom. It doesn't take a genius to know what's going on in your marriage."

"Those files," the chief continued, ignoring Maurice's outburst, "were opened last night and they answer a lot of questions. A phone call this afternoon to the police in the town where you and Ransom went to college together answered a lot more questions."

I heard someone gasp at that revelation.

"You went to college with Ransom?" Vera Rivers asked. "I never knew that. No wonder you were so anxious to help him out."

The chief held up a finger. "You haven't heard all the evidence yet. The encrypted files contained a photograph of Ransom and Maurice shoving a car out of a ditch. There's a young woman in the car, and she appears to be dead. According to the police report, she had borrowed Maurice's car and gone off the road into an icy pond. Ransom and Maurice provided alibis for each other, and it was ruled a terrible accident, but there are—were—two people who knew the truth. Three if you count the person who took the photograph, but we haven't located him yet."

"And you won't," the mayor said. "He's dead. He was a pain in the neck yearbook editor always going around with a camera. But that photo proves nothing."

"When Ransom emailed you that picture the day he died, your response via email is pretty damning."

"I won't be blackmailed," the mayor said.

"But you were for months. You were helping Ransom in exchange for him keeping your dirty secret. You were driving that car and that girl's death is on your hands."

"You'll never prove it. And you'll never prove I had anything to do with Ransom's murder."

"The thing about puzzle pieces," I said slowly, "is that they don't make any sense separate, but when they come together, they form a clear picture. You may recall the morning I discovered Ransom's body. The chief asked you to give me a ride home because he thought I might be upset. At the time, I felt bad about getting mud all over the floor of your golf cart. And when I stopped by your house the next day, your wife mentioned you had worked up quite a sweat scrubbing your cart."

"So?"

"I thought perhaps my dog made the mess, but I realized later that it wasn't Sunshine. The mud was already dry when I got in your golf cart. It had been there a while."

"When she told me about it this afternoon," the chief said, "I visited your wife and told her you had asked me to stop by and pick up your muddy shoes. She asked if you were doing some more gardening at town hall and I didn't have the heart to tell her otherwise. She went to the garage and got them."

"You went to my house?" the mayor thundered.

"The soles of your shoes match the prints in the photographs we took of the muddy footprints at the murder scene," the chief said calmly. "Right down to a notch in the left heel."

I glanced around the circle of people and saw emotions ranging from shock to grim satisfaction. Matt Riley looked cautiously thrilled, and I knew he was going to write the article of his life about this event.

"Ransom went too far, didn't he?" Chief Parker said. "Sending you that picture got a little too deep under your skin, and you decided you had to do something drastic. So you met him here, and when he refused to back down, you grabbed a weapon from a construction vehicle and hit him from behind. Like the coward you are."

"I'll have your badge," the mayor said. Veins stood out on his neck and forehead and I thought he might take a swing at the police chief. "I'll see you all in court."

The chief nodded, his calmness a direct contrast to the mayor. "You will. I can assure you we'll be present at your trial for the murder of Ransom Heyward."

SEVENTEEN

AFTER THE POLICE had taken away Mayor Maurice Bell in handcuffs and the Prince and Rivers couples had gone home, Grant turned to me. "I'd like to buy dinner for you and your family," he said. "Without your help, I don't know if this would have been solved."

"Eventually, I'm sure it would have," I said.

"I can't thank you enough," he said, reaching for my hand.

"I don't think we want to go to a restaurant in town," Aunt Minerva said. "Too many ears, and I'd like a little time to unwind before this news spreads through Champagne Shores. I suggest we go back to my house and order pizza."

Grant smiled at my aunt. "That sounds wonderful. But I'm buying."

No one argued with him about buying, and we piled into the assorted vehicles we'd arrived in. The mayor's golf cart sat in the lonely parking lot with Ransom Heyward's black luxury sedan. A strangely fitting end to their long and troubled friendship.

I drove Darwin and Tiffany in my hatchback, but my hands were tight on the wheel and I could feel the stress trying to fight its way out of my shoulders and down my arms.

"I didn't know how good a hacker you were until today," Tiffany turned around to tell Darwin who was in the back seat. "I mean, I always suspected, but wow. Maybe you should go work for the government or the FBI or something."

"I don't think so," Darwin said.

Tiffany and I knew from experience that pressing him on his reasons was futile. He'd spoken more and offered more opinions in the past week than he had in the past year. The poor guy was probably emotionally taxed out from all the subterfuge and interaction. I predicted that the gallons of paint in stock on my shelves would be adhering to a tight shaking schedule in the next few weeks.

"What do you think Grant will do now that his uncle's murderer has been caught?"

"You could ask him over dinner," I said.

"I would, but I'm not nosey," Tiffany said.

Over pizza, we discussed the case and all the evidence at length. Chief Parker joined us for a few minutes and told us the scene at the station wasn't pretty. He was calling in the state police to review the evidence and file official charges. He also asked Matt Riley to hold off on running his story for at least a day and to let the chief review it before it ran. The methods of exacting what amounted to a confession were unorthodox, but the evidence was strong enough to get a grand jury's approval on its own.

The only sad part of the evening was my aunt's concern about poor Irene Bell and her daughters. How they would handle the news of Maurice's ugly past and terrible recent actions was something none of us could imagine.

THE NEXT MORNING, I got up very early and put a second coat of paint on my kitchen walls. Lilac Dew was even prettier on the walls than it had been on the sample card. The second coat always goes on much faster than the first, so I finished in plenty of time to meticulously clean my favorite paintbrush, shower, and open the store at eight o'clock.

Darwin was already in the store and had a ball tied to a string. He tossed the ball and Tony chased it as my brother reeled it in. I remembered my uncle taking Darwin fishing once and only once when he was about ten. He'd declared the process of tossing out a line and waiting utterly pointless. I smiled, imagining what my uncle would say if he could see this.

"Good morning, Tony," I said, interrupting the kitten's pursuit of the ball by picking him up. "Have you succeeded in training Darwin?"

Sunshine slapped her paw over the ball and looked up for approval as if she'd accomplished something important. I petted her head and told her what a good girl she was.

"I'm trying to wear him out so he'll nap while I shake row two of the second shelf down," Darwin explained. "I was so busy yesterday and the day before that I got off my schedule."

I glanced across the street and saw Hazel leaning out her door and waving me over. I never knew why she didn't just call but being invited with an enthusiastic wave wasn't a bad thing.

"Be right back," I said.

"I hope you're not leaving," Grant said as he appeared in my shop's door just as I was walking out. "I was planning to kidnap you."

I saw Darwin's head come up sharply. "Figure of speech," I said.

My brother nodded and entered the stock number of a can of paint into his spreadsheet before placing it on the shaker.

"For breakfast and coffee," Grant said. "If you can spare the time."

I smiled and nodded. "I'll bring you something," I called to Darwin. "Maybe I'll surprise you."

I didn't look back to see his reaction, and I didn't have to.

"My hotel has delicious pastries from Hazel's shop, but I thought it would be nice to come to the epicenter of baked goodness," Grant said as we crossed the street. "And I have another reason," he added.

"What?" I asked.

"You're not at my hotel," Grant said. "And I wanted to see you."

I laughed. "I have my own place."

"I know," he said. He reached up and pulled something out of my hair. "Does your place happen to have a fresh coat of purple paint?"

"Lilac Dew. I needed a change."

We went into the bakery and Hazel was bouncing on her toes. She raised her eyebrows and pointed to the back of the seating area.

"You painted a table!" I said.

"I did, and I didn't even need to ask for help. I did it last night so it would dry in time for the breakfast rush. And it's a good thing because this place has been gossip central today with all the news about Mayor Bell being a," she lowered her voice to a whisper, "murderer."

"I don't think you need to whisper," I said. "Probably everyone in Champagne Shores knows by now."

Hazel poured two cups of coffee and put them on

a table by the front window. Grant and I pulled out chairs and sat.

"I feel bad for Irene," Hazel said. "She's a sweet lady, and I'm sure she had no idea what her husband did back in college."

"I doubt it," I said. "He was pretty determined to keep it quiet."

"And killing your uncle," she said, shaking her head. "That just showed his true colors after all these years."

Grant nodded and Hazel went over to the bakery case. I knew she would bring us treats without being asked, and I knew she would bring my favorite. Champagne Shores was that kind of town.

Grant clinked his coffee cup against mine. "I'd like to tell you about my next documentary which involves an entire community coming together to solve a cold case murder."

"That sounds just a little too close to home," I said.

He laughed. "You have no idea. I'll tell you all about it, but right now let's drink to true colors, beach towns, and justice being served."

"There are a few loose ends to tie up," I said. "For example, I should apologize to Mark Prince for my family's attempted trespassing in his garage. It's probably bothering him, and he has enough problems."

"I talked to him as we were leaving last night. I told him it was me and my associate Erin snooping around and looking for dirt on the murder suspects."

"Why would you do that?" I asked.

"To take the heat off you. I don't have much to lose, reputation-wise in this town. Especially with a guy who loathed my uncle, and with good reason."

"Thank you," I said. "Maybe someday I'll tell him the truth."

"And now, I have to tell you about my next film. I'm going to try to blend fiction and fact now that I can branch out with a basically unlimited amount of funding. The documentary will focus on the cold case, but it may also have a romance between the handsome out-of-towner who shows up to inquire about his family member's death but finds himself falling for a beautiful but curious local resident intent on solving the crime."

"That sounds very unrealistic," I said, smiling.

Hazel put two plates in front of us with forks rolled up in paper napkins.

"I don't know about that," Grant said. "Anything can happen in this town, wouldn't you agree, Hazel?"

She clasped her hands together and smiled. "I certainly think so."

I sipped my coffee as I glanced across to my paint store. Darwin was in the front window tantalizing his kitten with a feather duster. Sunshine stood inside my glass front door, waiting for me to return. Movement in my sister's beauty shop caught my eye and I saw her flip her closed sign to open. It was going to be a beautiful day in Champagne Shores.

* * * * *